Seize the Moment

With a bonus book included

"Being Neighborly"

CHERYL BARTON

Acknowledgments

I want to acknowledge and give thanks to all of the front-line workers who understood the assignment during the worst pandemic of my generation. There were many sacrifices made during the past, almost, two years and in the midst of it all, I hope this book brings everyone a few moments of being able to exhale and focus on something that will make hearts smile. We all love happily ever after stories and that's what you'll find in *Seize the Moment.* I added a short, sexy story at the end called, *Being Neighborly,* for those who love an extra little bit of spice in their romance. I hope doing my part to add a little sunshine to some pretty cloudy days will remind you that despite all that we've been through and are still going through, there is *love.*

I dedicate this to everyone who found themselves bogged down and locked-in during the pandemic. It is my hope that books like mine made getting through the rough times a little smoother. *Happy reading!*

Cheryl

Seize the Moment
Prologue

Finally! The garage door was going up and when Aubree
Campbell checked the time on her cell phone, which sat on
her lap on top of her favorite shorty-short, hot pink, silk
robe, the level of anger that fused through her was enough to
cause fire to shoot out of the top of her head. In the still of
the night, hearing the metal door open and then close again
was as loud as a bomb going off. That sound, mixed with the
idea of it being the middle of the night, an ungodly hour to be
coming home with no call or text with an explanation of
being this late, she knew that the man she'd lived with for the
past five years, Russell Hall was trying to slip into the house
yet again.

Her angst grew exponentially, not only because of his
nerve at doing so, but also adding to that, he literally missed
time with her the day before, a day meant for lovers;
Valentine's Day. She was livid and this time, she'd reached
her limit for putting up with his late night, middle of the
night coming and goings, with no accountability for his time
other than to say he was working. She had no doubt he
thought she would be asleep by now, knowing she would
have to get up early in the morning for work, but sleep was

the last thing on her mind.

Sitting in the corner of the living room where she would be able to see and hear him whether he entered through the garage or the front door, she'd been waiting for hours, even resorting to several cups of coffee just to make sure she wouldn't nod off and miss hearing yet another one of his stories of why he not only stayed out this late, but also missed the one day a year where he should have done everything in his power to make it home so that they could have quality time together.

Aubree shook her head and focused every part of her being on her hearing. Once the kitchen door opened, she shook her head and shook angrily at his attempt to open it without a sound. She expected to hear the sound of him walking across the dark brown wood floor, but that didn't happen. Realization set in that he must have removed his shoes before entering the house. He was *really* trying her.

Keeping her presence as quiet as she could, though she was fuming to the point that she wanted to scream, she waited until she saw Russell's silhouette as he crept across the floor with what appeared to be a large bouquet of flowers in his arm, making every attempt to stay on the plush gold-colored rugs that led to the stairs up to the bedroom level. If she wasn't mad beyond belief, she would laugh at his attempt to creep like a burglar. Letting him off the hook as he crept up two or three stairs, she reached for the lamp and lit up the room while illuminating his try at sneaking home.

"Really, Russell? *Really?* You're actually creeping into this house in the middle of the night? Thought I would be asleep since it's three in the morning? Surprise! I'm wide awake."

The low, monotone sound of her words even frightened her.

Aubree watched his head drop in defeat as he backed down the few steps he was able to get up before getting caught. As he turned in her direction, she prepared herself for yet another story about work, one she was not going to accept; at least not anymore. She was done with his excuses of why she spent more than a few nights each week in their bed alone.

"Aubree, baby, I'm sorry. The strategy session for the new show went longer than expected."

"On Valentine's day? *Again.* You're sorry. You need a sign that you can just whip out that has those words on it because you're saying them a lot more these days. If you stop doing things you would need to apologize for, you wouldn't have to keep saying you're sorry. What, you work with a bunch of men and women who thought it not important to be with their significant others on a day and night meant for love and instead chose to spend it working? Wait, or do you work with a bunch of people who don't have a woman or a man in their lives and so it didn't matter? Again, I'm last on your agenda," she fumed.

Aubree wanted to stand and come face to face and toe to toe with Russell, but all she could do was let her frustration show on her face and in the way her left leg shook feverishly up and down while crossed over her right leg. Her usual response would be anger after listening to his story of where he was and then she would usually decide to let it go, but not this time. This time, he was going to experience her fury. If she had to deal with it alone for hours, he needed to get his share of it.

"You know what this show means for me and my career. I'm going to be a late-night talk show host on a national platform. It's been a long time since a black man has been able to get in that slot on any of the three main networks. It's a lot of work, a lot of late nights and I'm sorry, but it's also taking up most of my time. It's the dream, remember? I thought you were in support of that. Was I wrong about that?" Russell asked.

Aubree's frustration with him shot up to a level where she knew there would be no coming down from. He was taking his lack of bringing as much focus to their relationship as he was to his career and throwing it back at her as if her annoyance wasn't warranted. It was more than warranted and he was about to find out just how much. She did stand this time, unable to release her ferocity while seated. She needed to let it all out.

"Don't you *dare* throw that in my face as if I haven't been supportive of your career. That's all I have been doing, but I thought I had a place in your life and in your plans and that I would get enough respect where you would at least think of coming home at a decent hour sometime or at least calling to say you'd be late. You took it for granted that I would just be here and that I would take any story you decided to make up on your way home to try and appease me. Not this time. Were you really at work or is there someone else? Yesterday was Valentine's day. Did you forget that? No flowers, no phone call, no text, no nothing. I thought maybe there would be dinner plans or candy on the counter or at a minimum a phone call. Perhaps a card, pigeon messenger, morse code, something!" she shouted.

"Well, wait a minute because I didn't get any of that from

you either," Russell retorted.

She laughed knowing he was going to try and deflect. She never thought she'd see the day that this would be his response to her pretty much saying he needed to pay more attention to his woman.

"That's what you come back with? Let me lay this out for you before you continue digging this grave for yourself. I called your cell and got no answer and your voice mailbox was full. Who's blowing you up like that? Another woman? I called your assistant, Connie and she said you were busy and that she'd give you the message. Either she didn't give it to you or you didn't care to respond. I wanted to know if I should plan for something special to wear out for a dinner I thought you may have planned. This one day a year, it would have been nice to have you plan something romantic. I do it all throughout the year. You had one day or night to plan something. You had one job and you failed it. You used to be romantic like that and then you got to a place of comfort as if you no longer had to do anything to show you love me because now, we're living together like husband and wife."

"Why didn't you call my work cell?" Russell retorted. "I think my personal cell was in my office in my suit jacket all day," he added.

Aubree wanted him to shut up and stop talking with weightless answers because if he thought countering with yet another excuse would pacify her, he was mistaken.

"Your work cell phone? I have to reach you on your work cell phone like I'm some business acquaintance? I'm not believing your stories this time. You show up creeping in here, surely to avoid waking me, your usual M.O. and what, you thought coming home with a gigantic bouquet of flowers after missing Valentine's day would ease my anger? I'm done, Russell. I've been putting up with you never being here, going days with barely a conversation between us and the countless number of nights you seem to find time to do extra work for your show, but not put in the extra work with me. I'm done. I've been here before. I know what this is."

"Oh, what, so now I'm some lame joker you've experienced before?"

"I know the signs and you should come clean and get it over with. Who is she? I hope it's not someone I know. What? She got Valentine's Day with you this year? Don't side chicks know that big days like yesterday are meant for the wife or main girlfriend and it's the day after that's reserved for the side chick. What? Am I the side chick? Is that why I get to see you the day after? You have some nerve treating me like I'm second fiddle. Are you using a condom? I know we haven't in years, so are you being careless like so many professional basketball players are with side babies popping up all over the place?"

"I'm not a ballplayer anymore and when I was, I wasn't messy, so don't go there."

"Oh, I'm going there because men like you come a dime a dozen. You think because you have a faithful woman at home, you can play your little games out in these streets and I would just live with it because you're Russell Hall, one of the greatest to ever play the game. Should I be lucky that you chose me only to get to this point where you don't respect me? You think that's okay?"

"Aubree, you are so far from anything sensible!"

"Now, I'm stupid? This just keeps getting better!" she huffed, infuriated.

"I didn't say that, but I guess you're going to hear what you want to hear and assume the worse like you always do. When does that get old, huh?"

"It will get old way after your lies. I know you're out here doing something, but I know you have friends who their wives and girlfriends dirty on the regular. What do you do, swap stories and excuses that usually work? Are you swapping women? I know the type. I know you're doing something and here I am, a fool once again, but not anymore. You don't seem to want to be here with me, so why are you? Why keep doing the same thing again and again thinking my reaction is going to be different? You knew what to expect or you should have. If you didn't you don't know me at all. I can't keep wondering where you are and who you're with."

"Then you shouldn't and you should take me at my word that when I say I'm working, that's exactly what I'm doing."

"Liar!"

Aubree screamed so loud, her words seemed to vibrate off of the wall. In her head, she imagining him laying with and loving another woman and she felt sick to her stomach. She knew it was happening. This wasn't her first rodeo with a cheating boyfriend. The difference this time is that he wouldn't admit it like other, bolder men would.

"You really need to chill, Aubree. I'm serious. I'm tired and I didn't come home for this. If I knew you would be all crazy and toxic, I would have slept in my office at the studio."

Now, she'd heard it all. They were getting to the grit of their situation. He was hitting her with honesty. He didn't want to be home with her anyway.

"This is just stupid and I'm done with you. I'm done with

us. I can't be a doormat for another man; not even you!"

"Doormat? You think I treat you like a doormat? That's not fair and you know it. Let's both calm down before we say words we can't take back."

"Please! I mean everything I'm saying and in fact, I'm done talking about this. I've done enough of this over the past year that I could bottle it up and sell it to other women whose men are treating them like you treat me; as if I don't matter."

"Baby, that's not fair."

"Don't call me baby. You can reserve that for the woman you were with before you came home. Do you smell like her or did you shower first? You know what, don't even answer that. I'll let you off the hook. You seem to have other places to lay your head and I'm thinking you need to make that a more permanent move or I can leave, but this relationship is over. I've put up with this from you for far too long. If I'm such an afterthought, feel free to not make me a thought at all. One of the guest rooms is calling your name tonight. Tomorrow, decided if you're leaving or if I am."

"Wait, what? Just like that it's over because we're having a little disagreement in the middle of the night? This is crazy, like I said."

"Do not call me crazy!" she yelled.

"I didn't call you crazy. I said the situation is crazy. I'm going to let you calm down and we can talk in the morning when you've calmed down. I have some show details to look over anyway. I'll be in my studio down here and if you want to apologize for accusing me of cheating when I'm not, you'll know where to find me."

When Russell turned to walk away toward the room on

the first level that he'd turned into a working studio and office, she quickly came back down the few steps she'd walked up and raced ahead of him. She wasn't going to let him dismiss her as if what he says goes.

"You have treated me like this for the last time. Tomorrow won't change a thing. I suggest you get comfortable in your studio or maybe there is someplace else you'd like to be. Man up and tell the truth is all I'm asking and you can't even do that. You'd like to keep me in the dark, being the dumb girlfriend."

"You were going upstairs, then go, but don't stand here to keep this fight going. We keep doing this and just as you're tired of it, so am I. I'm done with this conversation."

"Yeah, well I'm done with your cheating ass! We're done and I mean it this time. *Done*, Russell!"

Making her way around him, she made her way up the stairs, making sure to stomp her bare feet extra hard just for good measure. She could hear him calling her name, but she ignored everything he had to say as she rushed to the bedroom they used to share together, but where he no longer found a reason to come home too. Slamming the door and locking it, she threw herself on the bed and cried into the first pillow she found. She didn't want to end things, but what else could she do? She was done being taken advantage of, again, by another man – the story of her life with men. Maybe this would make him stand up and take note of what he would be missing if they broke up. For her sake, she hoped he would or she would get her confirmation that he didn't want to be with her anymore and if that was the case, her world was about to crash and burn.

Seize the Moment
1

Sounds of thunder crashing and lightening flashing outside of the bedroom window didn't distract Aubree from the pleasure of the moment that was happening inside of her modern, immaculately designed bedroom in hues of black, gold and white. Her specifically designed, luxurious and inviting tufted upholstered bed with its carved scrollwork accented headboard in black with gold trim was the perfect setting for night after night of titillating romance.

Candles burned around the room and the fire burning in the fireplace at the foot of the bed added to the ambience made for love. The satin sheets against her flaming skin supplemented the heightened pleasure of the moment as her body moved about trying to draw more pleasure fueling the fire within her that burned hotter than the fire in the fireplace.

Aubree moaned so loud that her sounds of pleasure drowned out the sounds of the thunderous clap of the clouds. With that sound in the background causing her own body to sizzle, she focused more on the light touch of her lover's hands as they caressed her soft legs, paying extra attention to her sensitive inner thighs. He was giving her the most tender touch, just enough of a connection to drive her mad with want, with a desire that could only be elicited by Russell, the man she couldn't remember a time when she didn't love him. She could feel his hands along with his tongue as he made his way up her naked body allowing his hands to move ahead the rest of his body. Everything else in her life was a blur and she didn't care because only this moment mattered. Her heart was beating rapidly with anticipation of what she knew was ahead of her; a night of lovemaking that would have her body shattering with salacious pleasure again and again and again and she was more than ready for it.

Aubree's body was on fire as she tossed around on the bed turning as she tried her best to prolong the intense feelings that welled up inside of her. Her hands clawed at the sheets, afraid to grab Russell by the head with her long, manicured nails in order to hold him in place the moment his mouth found her center when he urged her legs open even wider to give him room to settle in where he would make the sweetest love to her with his mouth, as only he could do. He was her heart, her love, her lover and her best friend. Russell was her all and he was giving her his all. She could feel her body on the brink of an explosion as her favorite song, *"Can't Get Enough"* by Tamia played throughout the speakers perfectly situated in the bedroom wall all around the room so that the music enveloped them from all points.

Being stimulated musically and sexually from Russell's focused and unhurried attention to her most sensitive areas drove her wild as her body, with a mind of its own, thrashed about in heat. Her screams echoed out over the sound of the music and that of the thunder as she begged him to give her more and as usual, he didn't disappoint as the dual action of his lips and tongue titillated her as wave after wave of pleasure cascaded over her. She lost control as her head tossed from left to right, hitting the pillows on either side of her head as she rested flat on the bed. Her hips rose to meet his face as his head moved up, down and around in circles, matching the action of his tongue. Squeezing her eyes tight, she felt herself flying higher and higher. The higher she flew, the more her body moved about as she felt Russell's strong hands holding her in place.

He worked her and worked her until her body began to slowly calm. She knew what was next as he began moving slowly up her body as she widened her legs even more and she was ready. Taking in a huge breath, Aubree held it in anticipation of the delightful feeling of him any minute now, loving her until she darted for that heightened state of pleasure again. Disappointingly, someplace in her head a phone was ringing. She pleaded for Russell to ignore the phone and give her what she needed, what she desired, but the phone seemed to ring louder and louder the more she begged. She reached for him, pulled at him, trying to get him to focus on being where she needed him the most, but then as the ringing got louder and louder, her eyes flew open as the moment was interrupted. She sat straight up in bed and reached for the ringing phone to throw it against the wall in hopes that it would shatter. Fully aware now, she took in what was really happening and realized, in the truth of the moment, she was alone. There was no Russell, no music playing in the background and no thunder or rain outside of the window making for the perfect romantic setting. She was all alone, the sun was shining bright through her bedroom curtains and she wasn't having some of the best sex of her life, at least not while she was awake. It had been a dream – a delicious dream, but still, it was all a dream.

She had been remembering and living in a time when she shared her bed with the best lover she'd ever had and now awake with the ringing cell phone messing up her dream, the reality of her situation settled over her while being reminded that a month ago, the day after Valentine's day, she'd broken off her relationship with Russell and she'd just experienced another lust-filled dream about him.

Sitting straighter in bed, resting her head against the headboard, she looked around the room and though some traces of Russell remained since technically, they were still living in the same house, just not sharing a bed, she missed his presence, but she dared not tell him that. A month of sleeping alone and she was already wishing she'd made a different choice instead of one made in the heat of the moment when she was again angry at him for his lack of attention to her.

When her cell phone rang again, this time she reached for it and sucked her teeth when she saw her best friend's smiling face grace the phone screen.

"It's too early, Jess," she said, referencing the nickname everyone called Jessica Blue who also happened to be her assistant at work.

"I know, but you said to call you if there was a change in the report that was submitted on the proposal for the design of the new office park and it's changed. I thought you would like to know before you headed into the office. I wanted to be sure you had time to read it so that you're prepared. I'm not only your best friend, but as your assistant, I have your back around this place and when you look good, it's a good look for me too," she laughed.

Aubree got out of bed and pulled down the long, silver, silk nightie that she'd worn to bed the night before. Wiggling her hips, she could feel moisture as it began flowing down her legs from the wet dream she'd just experienced. What puzzled her was where were her panties? She remembered putting on a lacy white pair before getting into bed.

As Jess talked, still filling her in, Aubree threw back the gray comforter and found her panties at the foot of the bed. She smiled to herself at the vision of taking the off in her sleep to give her imaginary lover better and quicker access to her womanhood. She was a lost cause, but wouldn't tell anyone.

"Okay, did you send the files to me already? As lead architect on this project, I want to go over every single change that was suggested before I sign off on anything else. We've already submitted the design through to the head of the project at the bank and yesterday, he agreed with the few changes I suggested. I can't wait to see what's different. Tell me this, are the changes major? Not saying it matters much to me because it's their dime, but I'd like to know what they wanted added or changed."

"Yes, it's pretty major, but nothing that would hold up the timeline of when the work is to start. It should be pretty painless, but let me know if you think differently and I'll have your team in the conference room and ready for you when you arrive. Should I expect you by eight?"

"Eight? What time is it?" she uttered.

Aubree reached for her iPad to check the time and was floored at the late hour. She was usually up by five, getting in at least a thirty-minute walk on the treadmill and out the door no later than seven. It was already seven and she was just getting up. Her alarm didn't even go off.

As Jessica talked, she took the phone from her ear and checked the alarm on her phone that was set for five in the morning and noticed it was set for five in the evening. How she made that mistake she didn't know. It was probably due to her preoccupation with the fact that Russell didn't come home the night before. It wasn't that he needed to answer to her anymore and since they shared the house, but not a bed, she shouldn't concern herself with his whereabouts. He was a grown man, free to come and go until he found a new place to live since he was letting her have the house; a house she would never live in without him in it, but she didn't fight when he told her he would move out and find a place and that she could live in the house until she found a new place and they could sell the house or if she wanted to keep the five-bedroom stately European style manor, she could buy him out. He offered to let her have it, but she didn't want to be his charity case. She would gladly find a smaller home, something more suitable for a single woman living in Los Angeles with a gorgeous view of the famous Hollywood sign.

"Did you hear me?" Jessica yelled, interrupting her thoughts.

"Oh, what?" she stammered out.

"I said it's a little after seven. Wait? Are you just getting up? Don't tell me you had another night of imaginary sex with Russell. I don't know why you don't just go down to his man-cave where he has been relegated to until he moves and

15

just jump his bone. You know you want to. Hell, I don't know a woman who wouldn't want to, other than me, of course because I'm your best friend and I would never do that and also because the hunk of a man I have does me right every single night!" Jessica cheered.

Aubree laughed out loud.

"Yeah, whatever. Not everyone has the perfect man like you do," Aubree declared.

"Oh, yes they do. You did, but we won't get into that. The last time I spoke my peace about you breaking up with Russell you took my head off and practically cursed me out. In fact, I remember a few choice curse words that I won't repeat right now. All I'm saying is, a month ago, we both had perfect relationships and you threw the towel in on yours because you were angry that he messed up Valentine's day, but you know my opinion on that – you didn't do much better either. We can curtail this discussion until a time that you don't need to be rushing to get a cold shower and head to the office. I'm in my car and on my way."

"I hear you and yeah, let's bring this up another time. I definitely need a cold shower and even if I wanted to jump on Russell just to scratch the itch, I couldn't because he's not here. He didn't come home again last night."

Aubree waited to hear Jessica shatter her eardrum with that news, but to her surprise, she got nothing.

"Is that so. Did he move already?"

Aubree couldn't imagine him doing that without telling her he'd found a place. They weren't on the best of terms, but they were talking. She spent most of her time on the bedroom level when he was home and he stayed on the main level. There was a lot of space and if they didn't want to run into each other, they didn't have to. There was a lot of that going on.

"I doubt it. I hope that he would at least tell me that. I know he's been looking at condos and was thinking of moving into an apartment that the television studio was going to put him in which is closer than where we live, at least that's what he told me."

"Since you broke up, he's been coming home every night or just occasionally?"

"I don't even know anymore. I mean, I don't stay up waiting for him or anything like I tried to do when we were together, but I can usually hear the alarm being disabled when he comes in and then when he enables it again once he's in for good if my car is in the garage. Last night, I was up reading until about two in the morning and he hadn't come in."

"Reading? Until two in the morning? You? Stop *playing!* You were waiting up for him. Just admit that you still love, miss and worry about him. I wish you would give in and tell that man you don't want him to leave. I know you and though you can be as stubborn as an ox, I know you still love and want Russell. Stop playing silly games girl and as your best friend, I can say that. Anyway, we can talk over lunch today, right? We're supposed to be going to that new deli not far from the office. Are we still on?"

"Only if you agree to not berate me about my relationship."

"No can do. I'm hitting below the belt and you deserve it so either cancel or get ready for it!"

"I'll see you in the office at eight and yes, we're still on for lunch. I guess I'll come with my body of armor since you like to hit me in the gut hard. Bye girl!"

Aubree hung up and threw her cell phone on the bed as her thoughts turned back to Russell. She wondered if he had found his way back to the house the night before and she just didn't hear him. She wouldn't dare go downstairs, to what Jessica called his mancave to see if he was there. That would look too much like she cared what he was doing these days or even *who* he was doing these days. The mere thought of the latter idea ticked her off. Could he be giving to another woman what she needed and desired?

Remembering she had another way to check, she grabbed her phone and pulled up the security alarm application to see if there had been any movement while she was asleep. She quickly entered her passcode and waited. Her shoulders slumped and her head dropped back when she read that her system had no activity since she entered the house the day before. He hadn't come to the house they were now sharing more as roommates than as lovers in a relationship. She had ended that. Throwing her phone back to the bed, she hopped up and stomped toward the shower knowing she couldn't focus too much attention on Russell since work was calling. Still, that didn't keep her mind from wandering to who he could have spent the night with and to the erotic dream she'd been having about him before the phone rang. She didn't know whether to be angry at his absence or happy that she at least still had her dreams of better, sexy times with him.

The truth was in her head, but she wouldn't speak it. She knew what she wanted, but she couldn't speak on that either. Talking about her feelings and those things from her past that got here where she was today, reserved and doubtful of others true intentions, even Russell's, was uncomfortable for her when it came to feeling and seeming vulnerable in the face of others.

Now wasn't the time to pity herself. She needed to focus and a very cold shower was the answer to that.

Seize the Moment
2

Another rough night. Russell was exhausted from all the energy he'd expelled the night before and only wished he'd had another place to put his energy besides into work, but like so many other nights over the past month, that was all he had.

At one time, he had the woman he loved madly and thought he'd always have her, but his last mishap a month ago proved that he had messed up and what they shared hadn't been enough to repair what was wrong. Since then, he felt like a wandering soul, going through life's routines, but nothing really felt right anymore and he had no idea how to fix that. He knew the answer wasn't to show up at his parents' house, yet again, in order to distance himself from his failed relationship by hiding out while he tried to figure out his next step when it came to his personal life. What he needed to do was find a way to get away from crashing on their hard brown leather sofa, which was too short for his six-foot four frame, especially when he had more than one big enough bed at his house that he could sleep in. He shook off the idea of one of those beds since Aubree no longer wanted him in that one with her.

As a second resort, he either slept in one of the guest bedrooms on the first floor of the house or the room he called his work studio where he went to relax with every kind of up-to-date electronic device and technology known to man. It was also his place to work quietly on creative ideas for his upcoming late night television talk show.

For the past week, he went between staying in his office, day and night and not going home and with his parents where he'd been for the past few nights. He knew that was his plan when at the last minute, as he was leaving the house after enduring yet another argument with Aubree, he grabbed a duffle bag and added a few extra days of clothing.

Now that he'd finally decided that it was best that one of them move and that it should be him, he had his Connie on the lookout for a place for him to live until he and Aubree worked out what to do with the house. He was more than happy to give it to her so that she wouldn't have to find a place to move to. Until he found a place he liked and one that wasn't too far from the studio where his late-night talk show was recorded, he would find places to crash. If he had the time, he could have easily picked a realtor and selected a place, but the talk show was launching soon and that was his priority. All of his time went into preparations for the show and now that he was close to his dream job, a career he left professional basketball to seek out, he was losing the joy of the moment because of his issues with Aubree. Her accusations and insecurities had finally gotten the best of him when she declared their relationship over and done with. This time, their fight didn't lead to an all-night sex fest which is where they usually ended up and they would then act as if they hadn't just gone through a trying time, but not this time. He was exhausted from work and from the back and forth and drama that Aubree kept bringing into their lives.

As soon as he thought that last thought, an image of her yelling at him came to mind when he realized the work priority is what broke them up and there was her accusations of other women, which were not true. Convincing her of that was taking its toll on him.

Aubree no longer felt like a priority when all along, he thought she was being understanding. He was wrong. Their disagreements, though much fewer than when they were in a relationship, after breaking up, she still found small reasons to pick a fight whether it was him forgetting to take his clothes out of the dryer, to leaving a half empty bottle of water on the counter after he forgot to put it in the refrigerator. She would complain about that too and ask why he didn't drink a smaller bottle to avoid having any left over. It was the foolish things like that for her to keep finding things wrong that annoyed him and so the night before, he decided he was too tired to have a fight with her in the middle of the night about something stupid, so back to his parents' house he went.

It had been a torturous month since she stated, vehemently, that she was done with their relationship and when she said he was no longer welcomed in their bed because she didn't trust him, he wasn't going to keep pleading his case on her insinuations. They had been having that fight for months and he was tired of having to defend himself. This time, she said it was over and he went with that. It never mattered how he tried to convince her that he loved her, she was a priority to him and that he wasn't cheating on her, she went with what she thought was happening and he didn't want to play the back-and-forth game with her.

Sitting up on the most uncomfortable sofa he'd ever slept on in his life, he rolled his neck around trying to ease the pain of the stiffness he was now suffering from. He'd fallen asleep with the television watching him, a horrible habit he brought with him to his parents' house. He stood and stretched while thinking about hitting the gym before heading into the studio for more run-throughs of his upcoming first night the first week of April. Though the show would be recorded during the day, it wouldn't air until late night, something he was still getting used to.

"The life you built shouldn't be this easy to walk away from."

Russell exhaled. He should have prepared for his mother's early morning speeches. For the last few nights that he'd stayed with them, she made sure to come give him a little piece of her mind every morning about how he's handling his breakup with Aubree, something he didn't want to get into, but he respectfully allowed her to have her say.

"Good morning to you, mother dear," he said, walking over, picking her up and planting a sloppy kiss on her cheek, causing her to giggle and swat at his arm to put her down.

"I told you to stop picking me up like that," she quipped.

"Ah, you love it. Doesn't it make you feel taller than your usual five foot three inches?" he joked.

"Don't try to distract me and change the subject. Did you sleep okay? I hope not because you need to be home with

Aubree working through your problems. Did you even try to work it out first before making the drastic decision to leave?"

Sitting back down, he reached for the remote control to change the channel, but not raise the volume. If he really wanted to piss his mother off, he would turn up the television, which she considered a rude and disrespectful act, so he didn't. He needed the few seconds to think.

"I didn't leave, at least not yet. We've been fighting for a month now, or rather she has been and I've been letting her get it out and taking it. Some nights I can't and that's why I'm here. I can't focus at the house with the constant yelling."

"So, you haven't moved out, but you're still planning to?" she asked.

Stella Hall was no slouch in the area of the inner workings of his relationship and though he loved her very much, he didn't want to talk about Aubree first thing in the morning. He had a busy day ahead of him and he needed to focus.

"I am, mother dear. We've been in a bad place for a while now and with our busy lives, it's hard to find the time to even sit down and really work it out. She's on a few new major projects where she's the lead architect and you know what's going on with me and the new show and my other businesses and investment. I've also been coaching and mentoring up and coming high school basketball players, something you know I'm passionate about and so does Aubree, yet here we are, the result of yet another thing about me that she wants to complain about. If she is done, then I can't stop her from wanting out of the relationship. I'm giving her what she asked for."

"Son, you've had disagreements before and you resolved

whatever was wrong. Why is this time so different?"

Russell turned around on the chair and spoke directly to her where she stood in the doorway watching him.

"This time, she really meant she was done and she's been repeating that for weeks. I've been staying in one of the guest rooms or my studio with no plan for us to share a room again. I shouldn't have to do that in a house I bought or with a woman who no longer wants to be with me. I can't make her stay and she doesn't want to hear anything I have to say."

"I'm sure you could use a little work in the relationship department. You have had a reputation that I shudder to even think about."

Russell turned his head sideways and looked at his mother as if she really knew about his proclivities with women before he met Aubree. He knew she had no idea. She was going by what she read in the gossip magazines and on line.

"You're talking about a time before Aubree and I was single. What single, professional ballplayer do you know of who hasn't sowed a few wild oats. I'm not perfect, but I would never disrespect her and she doesn't get that."

"But Valentine's day?" she asked.

He hemmed and hawed at another person tossing that day at him. He knew what he'd done and apologized but that wasn't enough.

"I know and I said I was sorry again and again. The day and night got away from me and I know I was wrong. I apologized profusely or at least I tried to, but she knows my heart or at least I thought she did. I was wrong there too."

"I'm sure you could find ways to do better and get your relationship back on track. Maybe if you had married her by now, you wouldn't be going through this."

Russell huffed out of frustration. Aubree never brought up marriage, but his mother did every chance she got. She thought marriage was the answer to everything. He always thought he and Aubree would one day get married and have kids, but for now, they were both focused on their new careers. There weren't too many lead, African American woman architects who were a stone's throw away from making partner at one of the largest firms in California. She fought hard to get there, just as he fought to get where he now is and he thought they were building a life together.

"I know you think that's the answer the world's problems, but it's not. Aubree and I would have made that decision together. Marriage had nothing to do with where our relationship went wrong and marriage doesn't make someone stay. It only makes it harder for them to walk away from."

"Like you're doing?" she asked.

"I'm not walking away; I'm being pushed away."

Russell was ready for the conversation to end. If it wasn't Aubree pointing out his every fault, it was his mother. He had hoped that when he made the decision to spend a few nights at their house, she would give him a few bits of advice and then leave him to the quiet space he always enjoyed when he needed a break from life. The family room was his favorite room in their house. There was the big-screen television in front of him, which his father had recently upgraded to an eighty-five-inch screen when he had the walls taken down to expand the size of the room. There was a fully stocked bar, though he didn't indulge often at their house. The night before had been a rare night and he was glad he'd gotten rid of the evidence of his night of a few too many glasses of Tequila.

"Well, I just think the actions on both of your parts is a bit drastic. Your father and I have been together since our teen years and when we have disagreements, we always work them out because our love is strong and bigger than any fight. You youngsters just hop around from one person to the next. Something goes wrong or if there is something about them you don't like, you just move on to the next."

"Mom, stop it. I have not moved on to anyone else. I love Aubree, but I can't make her stay in love with me. If she wants out, that's her right. I've always tried to smooth things over, but this time, she crossed the line and though I messed up, no one deserves the kind of wrath she brought down on me and the decision wasn't drastic – it was one I thought long and hard about over the past few weeks and I agree with her that the problems between us are unfixable and we've both agreed that separating is the best. At least we didn't get married because getting out of that would be a nightmare. I can't imagine having to deal with a divorce and all the drama that brings. We have enough drama of our own and this way, we can walk away without a fight."

When his mother sucked her teeth at him, Russell turned in her direction and smiled. He didn't need another woman frustrated with him the way Aubree was.

"You and Aubree would have to talk things out and try to work out your problems. Living together and not making the commit of sticking it out through thick and thin is too easy without being married. I don't understand why you won't fight to make it work. You and Aubree worked hard at playing house and now that your careers have gotten in the way, you're finding it easier to just give up."

"Mom, I'm sorry this is hurting you – the decisions I make in my life. Aubree and I have tried, but our lives are on two different paths when I thought we were building together to have the life we have always planned for. She's busy, I'm busy and things happen. At this point, it's no one's fault. We're both driven and we've admitted that we haven't taken the time we needed to make things work, but now it's too late. We're never at home at the same time long enough to figure things out. Relationships take work and we are in a different place. Busy lives have taken over," Russell explained.

"Wait – so that's it? Really? You and Aubree had dreams together *and* separate and once you've achieved your career goals, separately, anything you wanted to do together has perished? What kind of millennial mess is that?" Stella exclaimed.

"Mom, it's not millennial mess and aren't you tired of blaming everything on an age group? You wanted your kids to be successful in their careers and now that we are, you have a problem because we're focusing on it and thriving."

"Son, I love you and I love the strides you've made in the business world. You, your brother and sister have made your father and I extremely proud with college degrees and successful careers, but you have failed terribly in your personal lives, all three of you. I love Aubree, but the two of you worked out because you were equally driven to succeed and now that you have, you no longer have time for each other on a personal level. Your lives have become your work. I wish I could lock you both up in a cell and leave you there until you worked this out. You need a reprieve from the rat race to find time for each other and most of all, talk," she shared.

"There is so much you don't know or understand. Yes, our careers have gotten in the way, but on a personal level, Aubree has some issues with men that she has yet to work out and she's comparing me to what they did to her in the past and if she'd can't trust me when I say I love her, I want her and I don't want any other woman, there is nothing I can do about that. There are some things about her past that she hasn't let go of and every now and then, her thoughts of what happened to her in the past with men pops up and I become the many men who hurt her. If she's not willing to see me for me, what am I supposed to do? I won't be her punching bag. It's been five years and she's still hitting me with unwarranted jealousy and lately, her support of me has wavered. I've tried to share about the new show and she brushes me off because in her mind, I can't possibly be spending all of my time on the show. We're hitting the airwaves in a few short weeks and all she can think to do is continually ask me who I'm "*seeing*". I won't use the words that she uses, but you get what I'm saying. How many ways can I keep defending myself against her insecurities?" he asked.

"Until you can no longer speak."

"I've been doing that and I'm tired. She sees a woman look at me and it's my fault yet, I make a comment about one of the partners at her firm whom I caught lusting after her, even to the point that he licked his lips while eyeing her body from head to toe when he thought no one was paying attention and I'm seeing things. She declares she can't help if he finds her attractive. When I mentioned that, she went crazy saying I was wrong about what I thought I saw. I tried to tell her that other people will check us both out because we are, or were, a fine looking couple, but in her mind, if I'm not with her or running late or can't talk every time she calls or texts me, I'm doing something wrong. Her issues I can't fight."

"You need to find the time to invest in each other and stop making work your number one priority. I'm not saying give up your careers and chase the love, but I am saying neither of you have taken the time to work on you as hard as you worked on your career achievements. That's all I'm saying. If moving out and moving on is the decision you've made, then so be it. I know you hate that I keep bringing it up, but I want to be sure you are sure and that you've done all you can to fix this. I've never met a woman you've dated who was more perfect for you than Aubree. I just hate to see it end like this."

"I know and I'm sorry if you had high hopes of her being your daughter-in-law one day. She doesn't want a life with me and I think I've resolved to just go our separate ways and stop making each other miserable with all of this fighting. You can understand that, right?" he asked.

"I hear you son and I'm sorry if I'm prying."

"Don't worry about it. Where's Pop at?"

"He got up early to go to the store. Hey, did you see the news today about that virus? That coronavirus or something they're calling it? I hear it's worse than anyone thought. Are you being careful?" Stella asked.

"Yeah, I've been knee deep in news segments about it. It's pretty bad and you and Pop need to be careful too. At first, it looked like there wasn't much concern until it began spreading faster than the flu and it's deadly. Don't sweep this under the rug. I want to have a family conference call either later today or tomorrow after I get off work. I wish Brice wasn't living by himself in Norfolk. I think that soon, the college campuses will be closing and him and the other professors will most likely have to go to some type of virtual teaching and lecturing. I know he'll be good if that happens and he knows I have his back as his big brother if he doesn't, but thinking of him so far away as this virus gets worse concerns me. Have you heard from Leslie? Is she back from her last mission trip out of the country?"

His younger brother and sister were his world and he already spent countless hours worried about them, especially his sister who at twenty-two decided to focus all of her attention on mission work for the less fortunate in other countries. Now was not the time for her to be outside of the United States. He feared that soon, all travel would be restricted in and out of the country and she would be stuck.

"Oh, I forgot to tell you that she came back earlier this week. She called from her apartment in New York the minute she got back. We were talking about the virus just last night. I think she's planning on coming here so that she's not alone in New York."

"Good. I'm hoping to convince her to do that. I was going to call her later today to check in."

"You should probably stay put too. Trying to move in the midst of this pandemic may not be the best idea."

"I'll be fine, mom. I don't know what will happen, but I'm going to get my assistant moving quicker to find me a place, at least temporarily. Aubree can stay at the house, if that's what she wants. I need to get more into the news around this virus. I'm sure it will be the highlight of my show each night, especially if things continue to get worse. Let's do a family call to discuss a plan of action if this virus gets out of control. I don't want you and pop at risk and if Leslie comes here, I can get her an apartment close by. I know she likes her freedom and I don't think anyone should be here with you and Pop without knowing who is carrying this virus. Are you good with that?" he asked.

Outside of his relationship issues, he now had to deal with a pandemic and keeping those he loved the most, safe and that included Aubree, even if she didn't want him anymore. He still wanted her to be safe which is why he had no problem giving her the house.

"I am and I'm sure your father will be okay with that arrangement and I already know Leslie will love that. She's been trying to get you to help her get a place here for a long time and I want her close. If being here in California will keep her in the United States and not out of the country, help her get settled here. Brice will fight coming out this way, but we can at least work out a plan to stay in touch."

"I bought you and pop computers and you have iPads and can facetime us whenever you want or need to. We need to talk about what's next, so I'll call them and we'll work something out."

"I wanted to ask you how the clothing line is coming along? Weren't you launching your new dress shoe and sock line this week? I swear, I never would have thought that my son, who has loved wearing dress shoes and matching socks since he was a little boy would be the owner of his own men's clothing line that has surpassed the twenty-million-dollar mark in sales. Your father told me that," she said. "He still can't believe the money that can be made off of socks," she declared and they laughed together.

"I'm more of the face of my company and I make the final decisions when it comes to the design, but the day-to-day work is done by a great team I have in place. We're still planning on a big launch and I was going to do a publicity run in the major cities around the country, but we may need to rethink that. I'm hearing talks of a lot of the country shutting down by the end of this month which is in the next two weeks, I think by March thirty-first. We're still launching, but may need to do that virtually. I have meetings at the studio all day today about doing the show virtually just in case things close down."

"The show must go on, right?" she asked.

"Yes, it does. I'm going to get a shower and head into the studio. I'll call you later."

"Are you going back home tonight?"

"Yeah. I need to talk to Aubree."

"Good luck with that."

When his mother walked away, he grabbed his phone and sent his Connie a text telling her to find some long-term arrangements for a place to stay by the end of the month and to make sure the place had several rooms, all of them large because he would most likely have to do his show from there and not the studio. He was preparing for the worst while hoping for the best.

He then sent Aubree a text letting her know that he wanted to talk to her later in the evening if she was available. He didn't wait for her to respond. He left his phone on the chair, grabbed his duffle bag and rushed to get a shower. The world seemed to be going to hell quickly, almost as fast as his relationship and it seems, there wasn't much he could do about either.

Seize the Moment
3

"Aubree? Aubree! Are you listening to me?" Jessica yelled.

Aubree, now startled that she was caught unfocused on work, yet focused on something personal that was causing her distraction, she dropped the pen she'd been nibbling incessantly on and looked around the conference room, noticing all eyes were on her. Usually, she appreciated when she became the focus of attention around the firm because usually, it was for great reasons, but today, there was so much going on in the world and at work that no individual person was getting any kind of attention.

Everyone was worried about what was happening in the world. She was also distracted by the text she'd received from Russell that he wanted to talk to her about the house and that he was coming home later. She hadn't expected that. He'd been gone for several days, no doubt finding reprieve with another woman, something she'd been struggling with. She had no one to blame but herself for pushing him away like she did. She didn't think they would ever be here, about to be living apart.

Things had been pretty tense between them since the blowup back in February and even though they were still living under the same roof, they weren't actually together. She was nervous about seeing him later. For now, her attention needed to be on work.

"I'm sorry, Jessica. I am listening, I promise, but for a second my mind drifted to something else," she said smiling.

"No problem. I was going over the draft plan of what we're going to do if we are required to shut down. The partners provided some details and I was asked to read through them."

Aubree shook her head in agreement and this time, she would try and focus on what she was saying and not on her phone which she kept looking at, causing her to lower her head, a sure sign she wasn't really paying attention.

With the idea floating between her and Russell about him possibly moving out into his own place, she was scared that her hopes of them working out their issues would have come to fruition by now were slowly fading away. He didn't come to her to make up like he has always done and she assumed that was because her anger had gone too far this time and she didn't even know why she fired off at him every time she saw him.

In the days that he'd been gone, she found herself snooping in his home office and found some information on a four-bedroom, top floor condo in downtown Los Angeles. The place was magnificent and she knew it would be perfect for having the setup for broadcasting his show from home if the studio closed down, which it seemed was inevitable according to the news. Nothing concrete had come out yet, but she was expecting it soon. She didn't want him to go, but didn't know how to say the words. She didn't want to sound like she was begging after she fought so hard to push him away and now it all seemed silly and childish. The issue was, she'd done it and she couldn't just take it back. There last argument a few days ago had been over a bottle of water he had left on the kitchen counter and every time she walked into the kitchen that day, it was still there. She still couldn't understand herself and how she'd taken his head off over it. He was so angry that he took the bottle, opened the front door and threw it across their front lawn and then slammed the door. He stormed away after asking her if that was better.

"Aubree, we're waiting on your thoughts?"

When Dunston Myers, one of the partners of the architectural firm, Stern, Myers and Brown, where she worked called her name, she realized that she once again had not been paying attention and had no idea what he was asking her thoughts on.

"Oh, I'm sorry. I don't know what's wrong with me that I can't seem to focus," she said, playing off her blatant disregard for the conversation happening in the room.

"We understand everyone's lack of being able to concentrate, but with everything going on and the dire nature of the latest news reports, we need to talk about how we're going to keep things up and running virtually in case it comes to that," Alexander Stern stated as he stood where Jessica had been standing before he moved into her spot to take over the meeting.

Aubree nodded her head as Alexander spoke directly to her while also letting the other staff around the table know that he was concerned about the latest news reports of more cases of the coronavirus in the United States which has steadily climbed over the past week. Aubree knew, like everyone else did that soon, they would be getting a demand from the governor that all California residents remain indoors as much as possible to limit the spread of the virus that originally started in China, but had now reached across the world.

"Pay attention, girl," Jessica whispered to her from the seat next to her.

"I know. Make sure you catch me up on what I missed when this is over," she leaned in her direction and spoke.

When Jessica nodded, she turned back to Alex and joined the discussion.

"Alex, what are you suggesting we do at this point? We don't have a mandate from the Governor yet, but as you stated, one will most likely be coming out in the next few weeks. This virus is spreading like crazy," Aubree bemoaned.

"Well, as Jessica was just asking everyone, do you have what you need to operate from home around the clock? Of course, there would be no more traveling – everyone will be grounded and you'll need to stay connected with your clients. Business still goes on even in the midst of this. There are contracts that still need to be negotiated and new clients who need to be brought on board, especially those who have already approved plans for their designs. Everyone said they were good and we're just waiting on you," Alex said, as all eyes once again landed on her.

"Sorry about that. I'm good. I have certain files I'll need and notes from my office here, but other than that, I can access everything else electronically. I would like the computer and other equipment from my office. I have my laptop, but I like my office setup as I'm sure most of the staff does. Can we work that out? Zoom will help with facetime with clients and of course the usual phone and email thing, so I'm good," Aubree responded.

"Good, yes, we can get our IT people on that and with that, I think we're all good here. Let me just state that anyone who would like to go ahead and start working from home on a full-time basis while this is going on, go ahead and do so, immediately. The partners and I are in support of that with no question at all as long as you let us know if there is anything that you need. Everyone will continue to get paid and that includes all staff. You all have assistants, so make sure you connect with them about how to stay connected with you to assist you virtually. We're set up for emergencies. I know that some of you are worried about our announcement about the two open senior partner positions. We're still going to make the announcement on schedule in a few months. Amanda will be setting up weekly all-staff meetings via Zoom, which is the best way to stay connected to everyone and we encourage you to use that and any other virtual technology you need in order to get the work done. I expect the same level of commitment to your work while you're at home as you would give if you were in the office or out on travel. Our clients deserve that and much more from us, so let's make sure that the transition from being in the office and meeting them in person to being on the phone or virtual only, is just as productive. Aubree, Daniel, Suede and Joshua will be the lead junior partners during this crisis. Please reach to them before you reach to me or the other senior partners. Any questions?" Alex asked.

Aubree smiled and nodded, letting that be her acknowledgement that she was in control, though she could only admit to that being on the business front.

For the past few days, she had been on the brink of breaking down every time someone asked her about Russell and how he was doing or if they mentioned seeing all of the press around his new talk show. She still got the occasional person who asked her if she could get Russell's autograph for them because after all, before he began his career in the talk show arena, he was one of the top five power centers playing in the professional basketball platform. After playing fifteen years with the same team, he decided to retire when Hollywood came calling offering him a new career direction. She remembered him telling her that he'd had the itch to be in entertainment since his college years and now was his chance. Besides, he was tired of the constant travel and the wear and tear from playing ball night after night.

Aubree jumped when Jessica nudged her. As she looked around, she found that the conference room had emptied out and only she and Jessica had remained.

"Girl, where is your head at today? Still on the drama with Russell?" she asked.

Aubree exhaled and relaxed back in her seat, able to finally let go of her professional persona for a few minutes while she chatted with Jessica.

"Was I that bad?" Aubree asked.

"Did you realize you were still sitting at this table, staring at the seat where Chris had been sitting across from you? You have been out of it for a few days, but today was a major day of distraction for you. Is it all about Russell or does this mess with this coronavirus have you scared too? I'm going to work from home even before being told to do so by the governor. I have two kids at home and I don't want to bring anything home to them from interacting with all kinds of people all day, even those here at the firm. I'm not as vital as you all are and I'm pulling them out of school today," Jessica said. "What are your plans so that I'll know how we're going to work? Alex said we could all start at home immediately, but if you're not and you need me around here, I can make that work too."

"Don't even go there. You are just as vital as I am and yes, go ahead and start working from home as soon as possible. We already talk all the time, so we'll work it out. Just make sure you have all of the electronic files and all the equipment you will need. I know you have a laptop and other equipment at home already since you were already working at home one day a week, but reach to the IT department if you need anything else," Aubree encouraged.

"What about you?" Jessica asked.

"I don't know yet. I'm still working through that in my head. Russell may be moving sooner than I thought. He wants to talk about tonight and I believe it's about that."

"You still don't know where he's been staying the past few nights?"

"No. I guess with a woman. I told you I think he's been seeing someone."

"Lies."

"What?"

Aubree was shocked at Jessica's quick retort.

"You heard me. That man doesn't have a cheating bone in his body. He loves you and only you. You are just too foolish to know that."

Aubree stood and straightened out her navy-blue Veronica Beard, Italian blend pantsuit with navy and white striped top and matching navy Christian Louboutin heels.

"You know how men are. What about Mike? You told me he once stepped out on you and you thought what you had was perfect. I always thought he was a great guy."

"He was and he still is and that was a really rough time. We thought we weren't getting back together and we were on a break, so that didn't count. I had gone out on a few dates as well, though I wasn't ready to sleep with anyone. We worked through that rough patch and two kids later, we're still together. Even after that, I trust him because it takes too much energy not to."

"I don't know about Russell."

"Yes, you do. You just have a hard time believing that all men are not cheaters, but they aren't. You went too far this time. Russell is not, you know who, who will remain nameless while we are talking."

Aubree's mind went there and she shuttered at the remembrance of the man before Russell. That was an awful time in her life, one she would like to forget.

"I know I went too far; I do know that now and trust me, that was hard for me to say. I know we have our issues, but I didn't expect that he would actually stick with leaving. He's really doing it and I don't know what to do."

"Why can't you let go of old hurts and live in the moment with Russell? He's a good man and you won't find another good guy like him. Mike said the same thing," Jessica said.

Aubree turned to her.

"You told Mike?" she asked.

"Of course I did. I was hurting for you and he asked me about it. He said that the two of you breaking up would be a huge loss in the black love game and I agreed."

"How is Mike? Being an emergency room doctor, he's on the front line with this virus. How is he holding up?" she asked.

"He's doing good. He's decided to stay at the hospital and not come home to me and the kids to make sure he doesn't expose us to anything and of course, I'm worried about him getting exposed to this virus. No one knows enough about it to protect them other than to make sure they wear masks and gloves and be careful with their interactions with patients. I'm worried about him while he's more worried about us. This is all happening so fast. He was happy to hear that I would be home with the kids fulltime until this is over. I called him this morning when I woke up and told him I was going to ask about working remotely every day and if I was turned down, I would give my notice and then I find out that the plan was for all of us to be able to work from home anyway. This virus has me so jumpy."

"Me too and I was hoping they would name the new partners sooner rather than later. They need that additional leadership now, more than ever. I know they plan to promote two people and I have sacrificed a lot to show I can handle the job. Looks like we'll have to wait. Neither slot may be for me," she lamented.

"I say one of those two partner positions is for you and probably Chris for the other one. I know you're in the running or at least that's what I believe. The partners are very tight-lipped about their decision, but I think it's you. You have brought a lot of work to this firm, especially with all of the referrals from Russell from his connections. I hate that things haven't worked out yet with an announcement about partner, but they call you the ball-buster around here for a reason. It's because of your dedication and tireless efforts to make sure your clients always come out on top. That promotion has got to be yours," Jessica exclaimed.

"Whew, I hope you're right, but then on the other hand, I've been thinking about what I've sacrificed for this job and the possibility of that promotion to partner. Was it worth it? I don't really know. I've lost Russell in the process and I think we both have come to realize that we're at the end and it's all because we allowed our work to become the priority in our lives and as for me, I can't shake my jealousy. Have you seen him lately? I swear that man gets handsomer by the minute. I was in the deli the other day and the advertisement about his show came on and I heard two women talking about him. One commented on his bowlegs and they were imagining what being wrapped up in them would feel like. The other talked about how she would do anything for a piece of all that sexiness he was oozing. I hear that kind of talk all the time. Women throw themselves at him even when we're together. The temptation would be too much to turn down if the right thot made her play for him."

"Girl, listen at you with these fine man problems you got. You have one of the sexiest men on the planet all in love with you and all you can think about to complain about is other women wanting him? There will always be another woman who wants your man because besides being fine, he's powerful and he's rich. I heard on some news show that was reporting on him and they reported that his net worth was somewhere around half-way to being a billionaire. That means he's worth around five hundred million dollars and he still wants to work on the talk show, though we both know he doesn't have to. He's got all those endorsement deals, his clothing line is riding high and you told me he was thinking of getting into the wine business with some friends. What woman would not want your man? My issue is you're pretty much giving him away to the next woman because you can't believe he wouldn't have eyes only for you. Dumb move, girl. Dumb move. He's got all that security around him all the time, more fine men by the way and they're not going to get women get all up on him."

"Please, it's the security detail who provide the women for the men. Remember, Russell isn't my first leap into dating a ballplayer and all that comes with it, including loads of groupies."

"Those guys are as loyal to you as they are to Russell and stop trying to paint him as some panty-chaser. Let that go, girl!" Jessica hollered.

The reason she loved her friendship with Jessica was because she held back nothing when telling the truth and everything she's saying needed to be said.

"Men will be men and the hours he's away from home cannot all be spent at the studio. What is he doing well into the middle of the night? That can't be work. Don't you think it's another woman or perhaps, other women?"

"You've always worked hard and so has he. What's different that's causing the breakup because it cannot just be jealousy over his time spent away from you? You survived his last few years of playing ball and he was all over the country without you. I never heard you question his commitment to you back then. What's different?" Jessica inquired.

Aubree leaned against the edge of the window ledge that overlooked the downtown Los Angeles skyline. Being thirty floors up, the view was amazing and as she looked out over the city and then back to Jessica, she didn't have to think hard about her response. She knew the answer.

"We gave up on making time for each other. My travel schedule became ridiculous when I made junior partner and his schedule has been mad crazy, especially with a lot of travel, one time he was gone for an entire week. With that and the clothing line really taking off over the past two years, his mentoring schedule and just being gone all the time, our lives have turned into passing each other going in and out of the door. I can't remember the last time we took a vacation together."

"That's all? Girl, stop playing with this foolishness you're trying to get me to believe was what caused the end of your relationship. You blew up at him like you have been known to do and I bet he finally got tired of it."

Aubree twitched nervously hearing her own insecurities being thrown back at her. If she could be honest with anyone, she could be with Jessica.

"I thought we would make up like we always do. I had been missing him like crazy and then on Valentine's day, he completely forgot and I was jealous thinking he was with another woman. I really blew up at him and I mean like never before. I said a lot of really mean things that I can't take back like I didn't say them. We argue like most couples and then when we calm down, we make love and you know make-up sex is the best. This time, he didn't do what he usually does. This time, he agreed that we should end it and he was ready to walk away."

"No, he was pushed away."

"What do I do? I don't know what to do now. Tonight, he wants to talk and I think he's going to tell me that he found a place. I can't believe he's actually going to leave me," she lamented.

"You're a stupid fool!"

Aubree looked away from her and fell loudly into the chair she had been sitting in.

"I'm no fool," she replied.

"Oh, yes you are because you had the perfect man and you pretty much kicked him out. What if he has been with another woman lately? Are you kicking out any sex? It's been, what, a month? A little over a month?"

"Oh, it's been longer than that if you're talking about really good sex. He would hit me off with quickies, but again, our schedules were crazy and now this pandemic is crazy and we're all focused on that."

"Girl, who ends a relationship in the middle of a pandemic? Girl! There is a virus going around, a very dangerous one and you're mad because he didn't have the Valentine's day planned out that you wanted? Like you couldn't plan something. Ugh, women like you piss me off! Your whole life pisses me off!"

Aubree turned her back to Jessica so that she couldn't see the hurt on her face. Unexpectedly, she felt her head being hit with little objects and looked to the floor where the paperclips Jessica was throwing at her were landing.

"Stop that!" she yelled and then laughed.

"Don't turn your back to me. If this is how you treat Russell, it's no wonder things are messed up. You're being a child and not acting like a thirty-one-year-old woman. If you weren't my boss, I would really tell you off and then explain to you how you could fix your life, but that would be insubordination and I could get fired for that."

"Please," Aubree said and sucked her teeth. "I'm your best friend and your boss and I wouldn't fire you. Like you said, we're in the middle of a pandemic and after today, who knows when we'll be able to see each other in person again. I can't fire my best friend and expect her to still be my best friend."

"Yet, again, you can ruin a relationship with a man that every woman is willing to drop her panties for – the very fine and extremely handsome, debonair and hot as fire Russell Hall! Let me repeat myself – you are a stupid fool!"

"What was I supposed to do? He doesn't listen to me when I say pay more attention to me."

Jessica leaned forward and took Aubree's two hands into hers. She and Aubree had been having this conversation for the past month, ever since she decided that she would try and teach her boyfriend a lesson by breaking up with him in hopes that he would get on bended knee and beg her to stay. She played with fire and got burned.

"You were supposed to understand that he works hard just like you do. You and Russell are workaholics and I do remember you sending me out on a run to pick up gifts for your man for Valentine's day. How *suck-ish* like is that? Huh?"

When Aubree pouted and folded her arms across her chest, Jessica laughed at her.

"At least I got him something. He didn't get me anything until a day later."

"Technically, it was still that same night, just after midnight. You just didn't want what he brought home because you were too angry that he hadn't made any plans. If you weren't acting like a child, you would have gotten your gift and a little bit more, but no, you had to go to the extreme and now look at you, sweating it out with wet dreams!"

"He is still staying out all night and now, for nights in a row," Aubree whined.

"Now you're checking when he comes and goes when you broke up with him? You're not together anymore! Hello! Remember that?"

"We still live in the same house, for now, and the least he could do is be respectful and not stay out all night. Like I keep saying, he was probably with some woman. Why else does a man stay out all night if not to get something on the side?"

"It's not on the side anymore – YOU BROKE UP WITH HIM!" Jessica shouted and when Sylvia, another of the office assistants poked her head in the now opened conference room door, Jessica got up and closed the door to keep all nosey people away, especially Sylvia, the office gossip. If she were allowed to hear any more, Aubree knew her business would be all over the office by the next morning. She shook her head when Jessica made an attempt, by adding theatrics, to fake slamming the door in Sylvia's face after she had walked away.

"So dramatic and unnecessary!" Aubree boasted.

"I know you're not talking about me be dramatic and doing unnecessary things. Those are your double middle names. You are miss over-dramatic and miss unnecessary."

"Stop berating me and help me. I think Russell has found a place to live."

Aubree now felt like a little child as she stomped her feet in anger.

"Why do you care? Isn't he letting you stay in the house

that he's paying the mortgage on? I know you make good money and could afford that big beautiful house, but still, girl, you had a man taking good, good care of you and you get mad because of what? I can't stand you. If we weren't best friends, I'd hit on him."

When Aubree tried to hit her on the arm, Jessica jumped out of her chair and stood by the door, out of arms reach.

"Don't even joke like that or I'd have to cut you."

"Whatever. What's the problem? You broke up with him and he's moving out based on your wishes. What is your problem today? What can Sister Jessica help you out with today to fix your little miserable life?" she jested.

Aubree tapped her foot nervously on the floor. She'd never felt more vulnerable than she did at this very moment, but time was limited and wasting away. She didn't want Russell to leave her, but after a month, she didn't think there was a way to get him to change his mind. She couldn't take back all that had happened over the past month. She was at a loss, but she had to put her feelings out there if she was going to find a way to deal with them.

"Make him stay."

Usually at this time, Jessica would have a quip to throw back at her as part of their usual banter, but she knew Jessica was seeing something in her eyes that she's never seen before; she saw a serious plea.

"Wait a minute, we're not exchanging our tit-for-tat anymore are we? You're serious? Since when? Is it because you just don't want to be alone?"

"Neither. It's because I love Russell and I think he's finally tired of all the games I play. They used to work, but not this time."

"Girl, you can't keep a man in line with threats of leaving him. Eventually, he's going to do just that, like he's doing."

Aubree grumbled and tossed from side to side in her chair, angry at her antics.

"I don't know what's wrong with me. I can't do anything right. I can't keep him or break up with him right. What can I do? He may move out with the pandemic so that he doesn't have to get stuck with me for who knows how long. Help me!" Aubree pleaded.

She saw a glimmer of hope when an electric excitement appeared in Jessica's eyes as she leaned back. She could see the wheels turning.

"Okay, this is what you do and do not mess this up. This COVID-19 pandemic is a terrible thing, but you can actually seize the moment and show Russell that you didn't mean to make a hasty decision to end things. You'll only get one chance at this, so make it count."

"I'm ready. What do you have in mind? This better be good."

"Girl, when this works for you, I'm going to bottle this idea up and sell it so that I can quit this job and no longer have to slave away for my tyrant boss! Listen up because you're going to have to use what you got, to get what you want!" Jessica shouted.

Seize the Moment
4

After doing a supermarket run for his parents, his plans for heading to the office for a day of meetings suddenly changed with the announcement of the state lockdown or stay-at-home order issued by the Governor of California. Russell had spent the morning in meetings with plans to heat back to his parents for a while before heading to the house, but in the same day that he had been thinking about how long it would be before such a mandate was issued, he was now finding himself rushing around to get things done in order to prepare for not being able to be out and about like usual. He now found himself back at the studio for an emergency meeting to talk with his team before everyone began gathering what they needed to be away from the studio for an unsure amount of time.

Luckily, they had been preparing about a week for such an order along with his producer and production staff. No one was sure if or when it would happen and now that it was here, there were people rushing all around him.

As he looked around, everyone was trying to get last

minute tasks done before the stay-at-home order went into effect. There was already a plan to have all of the equipment he needed delivered to him and his team would walk him through how everything needed to be set up and the kind of space he would need.

Walking into his office, he sat down behind his desk and thought through his plan. What he hadn't thought much about was where he would be broadcasting from. With the issues he and Aubree were having and her obvious dislike for him these days, he knew the home they'd been sharing wouldn't be the ideal place. She could barely stand being around him now and he knew that the last thing they needed was to be locked down together not knowing how long that would be. It could be days, weeks or even months and the way she'd told him to leave, he was sure she would want him as far away from her as possible.

He was all set to talk to her later in the evening thinking he would have more time to find a place and move out, but now, he was putting a rush on that and would share with Aubree that he'd be out before the final shutdown and how he wanted her to be safe and to let him know if she needed anything since they would now be living apart. He didn't know how the conversation would go, but he was hoping it wouldn't turn into another blowout.

Ever since he royally screwed up, they had barely spoken to each other, and if they did, it was about issues involving the house, but nothing personal. And then there were more arguments than he could count when they did see each other. He hadn't gotten as much as a small kiss in the month since the relationship finally broke down. Things weren't at their best, but how it had gotten this bad to the point that she didn't want him anymore, he didn't know how he'd missed that. What was he to do now?

"You're here!"

Russell looked up as his producer and friend walked into his office.

"Hey, Brent! What's going on? I wasn't sure you'd get back here this fast for the meeting. I needed to pick up some things from my office since we have no idea when we'll be returning to record the show," Russell said, trying to now busy himself as if he wasn't just caught up in nostalgic thoughts.

"Yeah, I'm doing the same. After our meeting earlier by phone, I was pretty comfortable that we have a plan worked out, but now, knowing we have to put it in place immediately is a different story. Have you decided where the equipment should be sent that you'll need? I didn't want to assume the house because of what's going on with you and Aubree. Has that gotten any better at all? You're still moving out?" Brent asked.

Russell shook his head no to signify that things had not gotten any better.

"I haven't seen or talked to her for a few days. I've stayed at my parents' house the past few nights. I was already planning to talk to her tonight about me moving and now, I need to get things in gear before I won't be able to make a move with the lockdown. Being at their house, I guess you could say I was avoiding Aubree. I was tired of it all, so I packed a few things and took some time to visit with my parents," he said.

"She didn't know that's where you were going?" Brent inquired.

"Nah. I assumed she didn't care. That's been her attitude lately. Before all the drama went down, she found everything to complain about since the new year came in. If it wasn't an issue with me working crazy hours, it was about something with the house or really just about anything. The intimacy was pretty much gone since back in January. We've been going through the motions because it was expected, but nothing like what we really loved to do together. Even with that, she complained about me not touching her and when I try, she would push me away and that got old quick, so I stopped trying. I assumed she was stressed from work, so I let her have her space. I see that was a mistake because that led to many conversations about who I was seeing on the side and then she hit me with how I was back in the day before I met her. It was getting exhausting, so I stayed away. I did get a call about a place earlier today and I'm supposed to look at that tomorrow, but I hope to have at least one or two more options to choose from. I have to make a move quick and it has to be big enough to broadcast the show. It's happening in a few weeks. All of the promotions have been going great."

"Yeah, there is major talk about this show going global. I think even virtually, it will be a hit and we've been preparing for this for a few a year. We're all set and I don't want you to worry. As your producer and friend, I got your back."

"Yeah, now I just need to decide on where I'll live throughout all of this."

"What about the house? That's a lot of house for one woman?" Brent asked.

"She can stay in it as long as she wants and when she's ready to move, we'll put it on the market and split the profit down the middle. She can have everything in the house. I never thought we'd be here – I really didn't. I mean, I love her so much, man and I don't know when she fell so out of love with me. I'm not perfect, but I tried. I made a lot of mistakes but none that should have gotten us here," he said.

"I'm sorry to hear this is where the two of you are. I thought you were perfect together."

"Things were rocky before that. I think that was her tipping point. We were supposed to go away for Christmas, but I couldn't with the holiday programming and production planning schedule. I was supposed to go to her office holiday party and then we had that emergency programming meeting and I was late for her party. When I got there, they told me that she'd already left. When I got home, she had locked me out of the bedroom she was so angry. Christmas morning was a bust because she was already distancing herself to the point that I felt like she didn't want to be at the house with me. She complained that I probably had someone pick out and purchase all of her gifts. You know I didn't do that. You were here one of those days when I took off right after taping our dry run segments to go shopping and I didn't even do any of it on-line. I couldn't win. She had an attitude the night of the party you and your wife gave, to the point that she wouldn't even go with me, saying I couldn't make the sacrifice to go to her office party, so why should she make the sacrifice to go with me. It was becoming a major situation and it caused an even bigger wedge between us."

"Wow! Now we have this pandemic and you'll be going through it alone in separate houses – with her in the big ass house all by herself," Brent offered.

"I know and I'm worried about her. I called her parents

on my way here to check on them and they said they'd just talked to her. I wanted to know that they were okay. They live in an apartment in New York and I was worried. I offered to put them up someplace here in Los Angeles so that they could be closer to Aubree, but her father wanted to stay where he was. I'm going to work on getting them a delivery service to bring them whatever they need so that they don't have to go out."

"See, even with the breakup, you are still thinking about her and her parents. I really wish the two of you could work this out."

"Not sure that'll happen, but that doesn't mean I don't care about her welfare and that of her parents. I did a run for my parents today, but I then set up a delivery service to pick up and deliver everything they need, just in case I can't get to them. I also talked with Aubree's sister who said she and her husband and kids were doing fine. She also told me that she hoped Aubree and I could work things out because Aubree had dated some pretty bad and disrespectful dudes in the past and they loved how I took care and loved her. Too bad Aubree can't see how much I love her and would do anything for her. I love her with everything in me, but I don't know how to get that through to her. She likes to argue and I'm very low-key. I can't do the arguing thing. I'm not about that. I wanted to talk things out, but she wants a fight and I'm not going to give her one. I am worried about her with this virus going around. This is some mess this world is going through. How much longer are you hanging around here?" Russell asked.

"Not long. I have some show ideas I'll email you later about and we're lining up your interviews for several more months. We already have the premiere week guests and they are top of the line. The sports segment will be the most popular during your show and we have lots of athletes on a waiting list who want to be on your show, so we're good. I hope you're not worried about that."

Russell shook his head no.

"I'm more worried about my parents and my brother and sister. I'm having a family meeting with them all tomorrow."

"I hope you decide soon about your arrangements. There is a lot of equipment coming your way and we need to get that taken care of now."

"I'll let you know. One of my old teammates, Kenny, has a house that he's not using in the Hollywood Hills and when I spoke to him the other day, he actually offered that as a place where I could take up residence because he's planning to stay east with his family until a decision is made about the rest of the season. I'll know by the end of the month when we have to be indoors. I'm working on it. Either way, it won't be my house."

"I hear you. You're not going to try and fix things before the shutdown?" Brent asked.

"I don't know. I guess time will tell and we're all about to get a big heaping of nothing but time. I'm going to grab a few things and head to the conference room for the meeting. You good?" Russell asked, standing from his seat behind his desk and grabbing a box and putting in it the things from his desk he stopped by the studio to pick up.

"Yeah, I'm good. Let's connect this evening after you're settled. I want to go over that check list with our team one last time for the first show which will be huge. I want it all to be perfect, even virtually.".

"I got you. Later it is. I'm going out to the house for my talk with Aubree and if that goes well and not as stressful as I know it can be, I'll give you a call. I will say this, the pandemic has made me realize how much I love and appreciate her and if I've made her feel unwanted or unloved, I never meant for that to happen. I should have taken more care to seize the moment and give her more of the attention she needed from me. If I could go back and fix what has taken a downturn in our relationship, I would. So many are dying and are sick and I'm sure their family and friends would give up anything to have them back and they wouldn't let foolish arguments get in the way. I'm pissed that Aubree and I have allowed things to get this bad," he said.

"Talk to her. Talking is a great place to start," Brent said as he left out of the office.

"Yeah, we'll see."

Russell knew he would love nothing more than time to work out his problems with Aubree if she was open to talking and not fighting. Yelling, screaming and false accusations were not a way to a resolution. He wondered if they had enough love for each other left to recognize how important that love is right now. Every moment counted. This pandemic was definitely proving that to be true.

Seize the Moment
5

Unexpectedly, as soon as he entered the kitchen from the garage, Russell was surprised to see Aubree sitting at the island which seats eight, looking as if she had been waiting just for him. She was scrolling through her phone, but the television wasn't on, she wasn't eating or drinking anything – she was just sitting there. She glanced up at him when he entered, dropping his duffle bag on the floor by the counter.

"Hey," he said, checking out the fact that she looked as if she'd just come from working out. He was glad that one of the first rooms they designed when they bought the house three years ago was the home gym. That would come in handy for her with the pandemic causing everyone to stay indoors. She liked to work out several days a week, like he did and if the gyms were closing, she could still work out.

"Hi. How are you?"

"I'm good."

"Things are moving pretty quick with this virus. The partners met with the leadership team this morning and then the rest of the staff after we got work the lockdown was official for an undetermined amount of time."

"I know and things are about to get even crazier. The number of people getting sick and dying from this is getting worse by the day. The launch of my show is going to be virtual and my team is moving quick to get me all the equipment I'll need. I have Connie and one of my new assistants looking into some options around that which is what I wanted to talk about. Is now a good time?" he asked.

"Yeah, sure. Let me make one quick call. I'm going to be working from home and I'm having some new equipment delivered. My office wants to go over the inventory list to be sure they have everything. Give me five minutes?" she asked.

Russell shook his head before she stood and walked toward the stairs where her home office was located across from the master suite. He watched her as she walked away and decided to take the time to prepare himself for however the conversation turned out. He grabbed a bottle of water from the refrigerator before taking a seat at the island. He wasn't sure what her mood was. On his way to the house, he prayed that they wouldn't get into yet another fight, since he was about to tell her that he was going to move out into a friend's house temporarily until he could find more permanent digs. This is what she wanted so he was hoping for a smooth conversation. Things had been hot and cold with them lately; mainly cold. He still remembered a week back when he tried to get close to her in an attempt to reconcile before he moved out and things would really be strained. Gulping down his water, he thought back to one of their last big fights because since then, they have been doing a great job of avoiding each other. He walked into the kitchen thinking they could make up and he had no idea she would unleash her rage on him. He'd seen her like that before on several occasions over their five years together and each time, he couldn't figure out where such rage came from.

"You're cooking? What are you making?" he asked.

"Something for me," she responded without even a hint of warmth.

He walked around the counter and slid up against her in an attempt to nuzzle her neck and see if he could soften her stance. To his surprise, Aubree moved away, a few steps to the left to get out of his embrace.

"Okay, so I'm still getting the cold shoulder, I see. Okay, what am I still doing that is pissing you off? Is it my mere presence?" he asked.

"Yes. Are you still moving out?"

"Damn. You are really taking this to a brand-new level. You are getting more complicated. Now what is it?"

When she turned in his direction, the rage was all over her face.

"Who is she?" she asked curtly, catching him by surprise.

"Who is who?" he asked planting his hands solidly on top of the island and looked over at her confused.

"So, you're still playing games. You think I don't know you're seeing someone? Maybe more than one someone? I know there's someone and if you're not going to come clean, then we have nothing to talk about."

"Come clean? About what? About who? Why are you trying to make me say something that isn't true just to calm your anger? I told you and I keep telling you I'm not seeing anyone else."

She huffed at him and now he was getting pissed. He

hated being called a liar even if it was subtle.

"I'm going to keep asking until you tell me. Where were you a few nights ago? You were gone all day and pretty much all night and don't say you were working with Brent because I ran into him and some of your friends at that French restaurant you all like to go to that has that private room where you can smoke Cuban cigars. I saw the and to my surprise there was no you. I asked Brent if you were there and he stumbled over his words so bad that I realized he didn't have time to cover for you. Where were you? Who were you with? You come up in here rubbing against me tonight like everything is normal. What happened? Was your other woman not available to satisfy your needs tonight and so you come in here like everything is normal or have you forgotten the fact that we are not together like that anymore and you aren't entitled to this anymore!" she shouted.

Russell even watched her hand gestures as she waved them up and down her body to let him know that none of her would be available for him. What he wasn't going to do was take any more punches from her.

"You know what? Where I was is none of your business! How about that! You're right, we broke up so where I spend my time, you no longer get to ask me about. As far as me moving, trust me, I'm working on that. Don't worry your pretty little head about me. If I was seeing someone, why do you care? Who hurt you?"

"What?" she asked turning around, facing him so mad, that he could see her fists balled up at her side and her face was flustered and turning red. Her light-skin always told stories, even those she didn't want known, like how much

rage was building inside of her.

"You heard me. Who the hell hurt you so bad that for all these years, you've been putting me in front of the firing squad for someone else's wrong doings to you? I can't do right because even then I'm wrong. I'm out here building a brand and a future and you think my time is spent having sex with other women. There has never, ever been a reason for you to accuse me of that."

"Yeah – you men are all alike. Have a good woman at home and think she's stupid to what you're doing. You know what I've noticed?"

Russell knew this was about to get good.

"No, why don't you enlighten me since you know more about me and men in general than I do. Lay it on me," he said, opening his arms wide in a signal to her that the floor was her to break it down to him.

"You're getting sex from somewhere because for the past year, we were barely intimate one day or night a week when I know how high your sex drive is. When we met, you would tackle me several times a day, pretty much every day of the week. For months now, it's one quickie after another and that's cute and all, but I know you. If you're not bringing that type of loving home to me like you used to, who's getting it? You're always gone and I mean all the time. I thought when you retired, there would be more time for us, but there's less time than ever."

"You claim you don't want me! Remember when you threw me out of our bedroom, broke us up over some bull and then declared you didn't think we could live together anymore as you now patiently wait for me to find a place and move out, though I bought this house. The gentleman *that I am, I would never ask you to leave, so you can have it and I'll continue to pay the mortgage and do you know why? Because I'm sick and tired of your insecurities. I can keep taking the licks for all the men who hurt you and treated you like a doormat. We have talked time and time again and yet, you still hold a big part of yourself back, not wanting to let me in. I have to live off of the Aubree you want me to have and not all of Aubree like I deserve. I get it, you don't trust me, but that's not my problem it's yours. As for sex, if it's lack luster, all you have to do is say so. I've been working like crazy and so have you and our schedules haven't exactly synced up. Things aren't perfect, I admit that, but these accusations are just ridiculous. I come home, trying to be nice and sweet and you're already full of rage because what, you ran into my friends at a restaurant and I wasn't there? You need to stop. I don't like this side of you."*

"Well, Russell, I keep asking you why are you still here? Huh? Why? If I sicken you that much, why are you here. Just leave then! What you're not going to do is come up in here thinking you can rub up against me and I'll forget that you have been slipping and sliding with other women."

"Allegedly! Those are the tricks your mind is playing on you and there's no truth to it. Where I was that night? None of your damn business and you're right, I don't know why I'm still here or why I continue to try."

He turned to storm out of the kitchen and then stopped.

"What?" she screamed when he turned around and faced her.

"And just so that you know, I don't need to step out on you even if we aren't sleeping together. Just like I know you go through packs of batteries these days, up in that room all

alone pleasuring yourself, I know how to take care of my own needs. If you forgot, I showed you how to pleasure me with your hands, so you should know that I know what to do with my own hands, especially when my own woman wants to withhold sex and it has nothing to do with the lack of intimacy we've shared lately. That's not only on me. Yes, it hasn't been the greatest as it once was, but I thought we were in this together and you could have talked to me instead of assuming I'm with someone else. I would never think that way about you because as much as I enjoy great sex all the time, so do you. You don't hear me accusing you of getting any on the side."

"That's because I'm not dirty like you men are. I would never do that!"

"And I would? I'm done with this conversation! You'll never change and you'll never listen. I get a better response from the walls around here!" he said storming away.

"Then rub up against the walls then!" she hollered just before he slammed the door and tuned her completely out.

Those were Aubree's last words to him that day and since then, they had been living like strangers, doing their best to not even run into each other. That was easy to do with the size of the house they lived in.

He heard her coming back toward the kitchen just as he'd finished going over the last big fight they'd had. They said some hurtful things and neither had yet to apologize. He wanted to do that for the entire week, but every time he did see her, she would practically snarl at him. He decided it was best to leave her alone and spend as little time as possible at the house. After they talked, she wouldn't have to worry about him being in her space anymore.

"Sorry about that. I was waiting for a text that they were ready to go over the equipment and delivery schedule with me and I got the text just as you walked in. You still want to talk?" she asked.

"Yes, let's sit at the table," he said, gesturing for her to join him at the large round, dark brown wood table that sat six. He sat across from her. "I want to talk about me moving out. I know we haven't communicated much these days, but we can't go on like this under the same roof and barely speaking. We walk around here like we don't know each other and that hurts. I don't know how you feel about that, but our time together meant something to me – enough that this place we're in is more than either of us should have to deal with daily. There is a nasty pandemic happening in the world that no one can seem to explain or get a grip on. In a few days, we won't be able to go out to work, eat or visit others. We'll all be locked in and based on our interaction lately, being locked in together is a bad idea."

"Well," Aubree started to interrupt.

"Let me finish first. I've been thinking about this most of the week and more today. Kenny is on the east coast where he intends to stay with his family since the basketball season has come to a screeching halt. He's offered to let me stay at his house, which is just as big as ours, and it would be good for me to broadcast my show live. There is a lot of sunlight and windows with a back yard that overlooks the mountains like our house does. My team is willing to still do the show, but safely from a large motorhome we'll add to the property for the technology to be run out of. Brent, since he doesn't live far, will work with me to keep our list of guests coming and we're planning a large launch party for next week, on

April first. That's what I've been busy doing. It's a lot to launch a new television show, especially a night time talk show competing against the Jimmy's who have taken over late-night television. This has been a year in the making and it's finally here. I wish you could be happy for me, but I understand."

"I am happy for you. I'm proud of what you've accomplished," she said.

Russell heard and felt something different in her voice. She didn't appear to be on the edge of ripping into him. Nor was she acting like she couldn't care what he was talking about. He did expect her response to be one on impatience, since that was what he'd been getting from her lately.

"Thank you. I think I'm going to take him up on his offer. I'm still working on finding a more permanent place to live. I was thinking of a condo at first, but now with the show going virtual, I realize I'll need more space, so I'm looking for a house. That will take some time especially with what's going on in the world. We'll need to talk about this house and what to do with it. I think you should stay here through the pandemic because I think you'd be safer. I would feel better knowing you were safe because I don't know how crazy people are going to get. Will there be an increase in crime, looting of closed stores, people thinking this is some kind of apocalypse and checking out people's homes. The only way I know to keep you safe is if you are in this house that can be locked down like Fort Knox. I'm increasing security around the property around the clock and someone is going to come out tomorrow to make sure there are no problems with it. If you need me for anything, you'll know how to reach me, that is if you want to. I just want and need to know that you're safe in this house alone. I checked in with your parents and they're good and so are mine. I stopped at the store and really stocked their freezer and pantry. I'm going to do a run for this house in a few minutes. Let me know what you need. Some things are hard to get because people know the lock down is coming, but I will get what I can. I'm going to have the fellas help me move my stuff out at the end of the week. I picked up some boxes on my way home. If you want me to do that when you're not here, let me know and we can work it out. I'm sorry we didn't work out. I didn't know things were so bad that you would be done with me all together. I would never, ever purposely hurt you or do something as underhanded and dirty as cheat on you to get sex when I know I can get the best sex of my life with you; at least I used to."

He wanted to say more, but let the rest of what he was going to say just live in his head. He put everything that he'd been thinking out for her to hear and now he waited. He searched her eyes and didn't see anger. If he could speak the word out loud, he would almost say her eyes read of compassion. He was giving her what she wanted so that may be why she wasn't flying off the handle at him.

Seconds and then minutes went by as she looked everywhere in the kitchen but at him. Her hands moved about nervously on the table. She crossed and uncrossed her legs and shifted around in her seat as if she couldn't keep still. Thinking she wasn't going to respond, he moved to get up and she cleared her throat.

"Wait," she said softly.

Russell leaned back in his chair and waited.

"First of all, thanks for everything you just said,

especially for checking in with my parents. You didn't have to do that."

"Yes, I did. I still love them and care about them and I want them to be safe."

"And me – you're looking out for me too and I appreciate that."

"You've always been my priority, even if you didn't know it or felt like that was the case. These are unprecedented times. This virus is killing people and others with mental illnesses will be triggered and may do desperate things. I couldn't live if anything happened to you."

"About the living arrangements. You shouldn't have to deal with moving everything and finding a temporary house and then a permanent house. Your show is about to launch in a week and I know this house has all that you'll need. I know Kenny has offered you his house, but you already have a house. I think we can survive what's happening in the world by doing so under the same roof at least until this virus mess is over. I can't see it taking more than a few weeks. Maybe it will come and go like flu season does each year. There is plenty of breathing room here and you are already focused on your show and don't need the stress of moving and getting everything done by the lock down date. Have your equipment delivered here. We'll make it work. I don't want you out there just like you don't want me out there. You should be here just like I should be. I know we've been toxic for some time now, but we can make this work. I hope you'll think about it and realize it's the best decision."

"Us, here, together under the same roof with all the fighting we keep doing?" he asked.

"Okay, I will admit that I've been a hothead, but I really

want to be supportive of this new step in your career and you and me both know if your show has to be virtual, no other place will have what you need like this property. We overlook some beautiful mountains and the electrical grid will be able to accommodate the extra power you will need for the equipment and the van or bus that you plan to have on the property and besides, his house doesn't have the security this house has. You should be here. What do you say or do you want to think about it?"

Wow, was all he could think. Aubree came from left field with that suggestion. After weeks of pretty much making sure he knew that she hated him and couldn't stand to be with him, she was inviting him to stay with her throughout the pandemic. He would like nothing more than to stay where he would have to make little effort to prepare for the lock down. She was right about how viable their own house would be for his show's production and he wouldn't have to worry about not having sufficient resources if he took Kenny up on his offer to use his house. They were together for five years and though lately, it's been rough, he believed they could live together but separate under the same roof.

"If you're sure you'd be good with that."

"I'm one hundred percent sure. Are you staying?" she asked.

"Yeah, I am. Can we agree to no fighting? I get that we're over and unlike last week, I promise to not push up on you and I'll stay out of your hair as much as I can. Our offices are on two different floors so that will make it sort of easy. If I'm in your way, just tell me, okay?"

"Okay."

"Well, I have some calls to make myself and write down a

list of things you want me to get from the store, especially food. I don't know if we'll be able to get delivery or not though I'm sure supermarkets will stay open. Some stores are essential like gas stations and food stores and hopefully liquor stores. I need to stock up on that," he joked.

"That will be first on my list of things. You sure you don't mind?" Aubree asked.

"I don't mind at all."

"I'll look through the fridge and the one in the garage and check the deep freezer. I already know what's needed in the pantry. I was going through that before you got ho...*here*."

Too late, Russell thought. She was about to say before he got home and she changed it to here. He guessed her saying home was too much like what their life was before they broke up. He would let it slide. When she stood, he did also and went toward his office while she walked toward the garage where they kept an extra refrigerator, freezer and smaller pantry. He wanted to say something else. He felt like more needed to be said, but with them now deciding to stay under the same roof, there would be time to talk more if they needed to. He could only hope that they wouldn't live in the house together in total silence. That would be worse than him moving out.

Seize the Moment
6

Three weeks in and Aubree was going crazy over being stuck in the house for most of the day. There really wasn't any place to go. Her usual spots were all closed and all of her friends were staying close to home. She did go out every day to walk around their property to get some outside exercise and sun.

She, like the rest of the world were embroiled in the fact that the virus was ravaging not just the United States, but the entire world. Each day, the news brought the latest numbers of people getting sick and dying and thankfully her family and friends were all being safe. She had daily facetime chats with her parents and she even spoke to Russell's mother several times a week. Thankfully, there were no hard feelings over the drama with her and Russell that impacted her close relationship with his parents just as he still maintained a good relationship with her parents. Neither set of parents understood why they were still saying they were broken up when they still lived in the same house. Everyone was confused and at this point, so was she. Three weeks and though she and Russell actually had little interaction with each other, she did watch the launch of his new talk show from their family room with the large screen television and surround sound. She had watched from a distance as his team set everything up that he would need. There were two trailers on their property where his team worked from and on a few occasions, had even spent the night there. Only Brent was allowed in the house and he had to wear a mask and gloves. All of the guests, starting with the show's premiere episode joined Russell virtually from their homes and that included his musical guests. There were professional players in every sport imaginable on his show with more negotiating with their agents to get on. He had the top musical guests in the world being interviewed and singing their hit songs. The biggest surprise was when he received surprise virtual visits and congratulations from his competing talk show hosts. That made his night on the first night. Since then, Russell had been so busy working on production and fine-tuning the virtual experience that she rarely ran into him.

Most troublesome was that he didn't appear to care that they were no longer together though they were under the same roof. She thought that they would find their way back to each other if they were locked down together, but so far, other than a few greetings here and there or running into each other in the kitchen or in the gym, she pretty much stayed to the upper level while he stayed on the first level.

On the last day before the lockdown, she had gone out to grab a few last-minute things at the store and returned to find that he had moved all of his clothes and other items out of the bedroom they had shared and into one of the guest rooms on the first floor. When she saw his empty closet, which was across from hers right off the master bedroom, she suddenly felt lonely and was missing him like crazy. His empty closet made it all real that he had resigned himself to her desires that they were no longer a couple. How could she tell him that she changed her mind? She had been thinking again and again about what Jessica told her about using her womanly power, the one between her legs to get back into his graces by getting him back into bed. At this point, she didn't know if that would work because the last time he tried to touch her, she refused him and moved away from him as if he were a leper. She now regretted doing that but that thing called pride wouldn't allow her to apologize. Something in her wouldn't let her beg him to take her back and give her another chance. She didn't know what to do as she paced around her bedroom after getting off work. She'd spent the entire day in one meeting after the other. She could hear Russell moving around in the kitchen and thought maybe this would be a good time to see if they were on better speaking terms. She hated the distance between them even though it was happening because of her.

Checking her form in the mirror, she felt like she was already gaining weight and promised she work out more. Her hair was pinned up and she had on a pair of leggings and a long t-shirt she'd picked up from Disneyland months ago when everything was still open. She still couldn't believe that even that place was closed to the public. She couldn't remember another time where that had ever happened before.

So much about the world was changing and with it, she felt like she was changing too and because of that, she began to see how she had been taking Russell's love for granted and then throwing it back in his face. Now, when she really wanted him the most, she wasn't the type of woman to beg and plead, which left her at a crossroad of what to do. Maybe if she went down to the kitchen and ended up there the same time as him, especially if he was cooking, maybe a conversation longer than hi and hello would ensue. It was worth a shot.

Adding a light lip gloss and some eyeliner, she headed downstairs. Walking slowly down each of the stairs of the spiral stair case, she felt like she was sneaking around in her own house. She was about to make herself known to Russell just before reaching the kitchen until she heard him whispering softly into the phone. To her, his tone was sexy and alluring in a way that was used to engage with her. She could hear him uttering words about sex and orgasms and when he turned his head to the side, she could see his bright, alluring smile as if the woman on the other end of the phone could see and hear him. Someone was making him smile in a way that she hadn't seen in a very long time. She used to make him that happy.

"Phone sex?" she heard him say.

Was he making a date for phone sex with someone? She would not embarrass herself by walking in on that. She wanted to bolt and run back to her room. She knew she never should have thought that they could have something again. She was close to believing his words that he never cheated on her until she heard him utter the words, phone sex. That had to be a woman.

Turning, she forgot about the tall, floor plan to her left and she knocked it over. Trying her best to pick it up and run, she didn't make it far when Russell saw her and called after her as she tried to rush to the stairs.

"Aubree? I know you hear me!" he shouted. "Hold on a second."

"No. Go ahead and finish talking to whoever that woman is. I knew you were lying."

She made it as far as the steps when she heard him rushing toward her.

"Aubree, stop! Stop running away from me as if you detest the idea of being near me," Russell hollered and she stopped moving up the steps to what she knew would be freedom from embarrassment. Here she was coming downstairs to try and work her way back into his life and he was on the phone with another woman, most likely uttering words of seduction to her. How could she have been so stupid to think that he would be interested in her anymore? If it wasn't for this pandemic that kept them inside around the clock, he would be living in his own place by now.

"How could you? I didn't think you would do this, talking about phone sex with some woman while I'm here. I know we're not together, but I thought you would be more discreet than this!" she declared and prepared to run from him again. "I didn't mean to sneak up on you and interrupt your phone conversation. It sounded pretty intense and I'm sure she doesn't need me interrupting your time with her considering the circumstances," she said.

"Come here, Aubree," Russell said.

"But, you're on the phone," she tried to whisper.

"Come here, Aubree," he repeated.

Moving slowly on legs that seemed to wobble uncontrollably, she moved closer to him, wrapping her arms tight around her body.

"I really should get back upstairs," she whispered.

"Why are whispering?" he asked.

"Because, you're on the phone with a woman and I don't need her talking about me being here while you're talking to her about sex. I heard what you were saying and it was pretty steamy," she stammered out.

"Oh, really? Steamy? Here," Russell said handing her his cell phone.

Aubree stepped back and waved the phone away.

"I will not! I'm going back upstairs," she said.

"Aubree, take the phone and say hello."

"Is this what we're doing now? Messing with each other's heads?"

"Aubree, if you don't take this phone, stop being so stubborn and say hello!" Russell demanded and smiled at her.

With shaky hands, she took the phone and keeping her eyes on him, she spoke softly.

"Hel..Hello?" she questioned.

"Aubree my belle! How are you? I love you and I wouldn't let that fool be on the phone talking to a woman like that. We're just going over the content in the book of an author who wants to be on his show that I went to college with. I promised I'd get her a sit down with my big brother," Brice said.

"Brice? He's talking to you? I thought you were a woman," she said, looking at Russell and now, more embarrassed than ever.

"Heck no. That man is madly in love with you and if I thought he was trying to sweet talk another woman, I would beat him down and then steal you away from him."

Aubree laughed so loud, she had to cover her mouth with her hand.

"You are crazy. Are you staying safe?" she asked.

"Okay, I didn't mean for the two of you to have a long conversation. I wanted you to see that I wasn't talking to a woman. When will you realize that I'm not hiding anything or seeing anyone, pandemic or not?"

"Russell is questioning the section of her book she wants to read out loud to the virtual audience and it's pretty steamy. He wants her to pick something else. He was reading the pages to me and I had no idea they were that steamy."

When she looked to Russell, who clearly could hear what Brice was saying, he held up the steamy romance novel that she couldn't see with his back to her as he stood in the kitchen.

"Oh, I see."

"How are you doing putting up with this fool during a pandemic? I can come take care of him and hide the body if he isn't treating you right," he joked, causing her to laugh even harder at the visual.

"Brice, Russell would lay you out flat on your back if you even tried anything. I'm good. You make sure you're staying safe. I'm going to give the phone back to Russell," she said.

"Brice, let me hit you back and I'll think about it. I need to pass this to my producer, but note that if I agree to this, she'll only get a few minutes and the part she reads needs to be a little tamer than this. I can't have her on my show talking about phone sex and all the things she has here that came after those words. Let me read more of this and I'll hit you back tomorrow. Check on your sister. I spoke to her last night and she's happy to be here in Los Angeles. You moved quick to get her out of New York. That place has it worse than any other state right now. I think it's because of those close quarter apartments, what many all the concrete jungle. I was a little hesitant about her staying with mom and dad, but she promised me that she wouldn't be out and about with old friends, realizing that the number one priority is keeping them safe and herself also."

"Cool. I talked to her last week, but I'll call her in a few. Either kiss that beautiful woman named Aubree for me or the next time I see her, I'm going to officially steal her away from you. She's too good for you anyway!" Brice chimed.

"Yeah, from your lips to God's ears! Later, bro."

When Russell's eyes landed on her, Aubree didn't know if she should run or stay. His eyes were so penetrating that she couldn't do anything but stand there looking at him.

"I didn't mean to disturb you," she said.

"You weren't disturbing me, but why did you run away? It was because of what you heard? Stop thinking I'm messing around, even though, technically, that's not what it would be at this point. What will it take for you to let go of that? A lie detector test? What is it? I can't deal with you throwing that at me every chance you get. You must have come down for something. This isn't the first time you've come down and thought I wasn't aware of you. I'm always aware of you. I can sense your presence even before you arrive. I'm that in-tuned to you."

"I was coming to fix me something to eat."

"Yet, you're still on the steps. Not hungry anymore? I'm

about to make myself a hoagie. Do you want one?" he offered.

"No, I don't want the bread. I think I'll just have some fruit for now and cook something later."

"I wouldn't talk to another woman while I'm here, not on the level that you're thinking. I can't say that I won't find myself with another woman since you took yourself out of the running, but it's not going to happen just like that. I can't turn my feelings on and off for you like you apparently can and that's not a criticism; it's fact. Come on. There's enough room in the kitchen for us both."

Aubree nodded her head and followed him back toward the kitchen, checking out the fact that he had on a pair of his old team ball shorts and no shirt. His body was so chiseled and in shape that she felt tingly all over just watching him walk. The curve of his legs made her shiver as she walked. She was reminded of just how perfect his toned ass was.

She thought about the many personal toys she had in her room, most which Russell had bought her and how none of them were doing her justice when she knew that Russell had over nine inches that brought her please again and again, even with his spicy and extra X-rated quickies. She was in dire need of one now.

Now that they were together all the time and this is what she had been longing for, they weren't even together. Her timing sucked!

Walking into the kitchen, she went straight for the refrigerator and then turned and watched as he made one of the largest subs she'd ever seen.

"Are you really going to eat that?" she asked him.

"I am."

"You're going to wipe the counter off, right? I see a lot of crumbs already."

"Really, Aubree? I'm hungry and now is not the moment for you to find little things to complain about. Crumbs on the counter while I'm actually making my sandwich? That's pretty much going to happen. I promise on my boy scout oath that I will wipe the counter down until it shines with perfection. Is that good?"

If it weren't for his brusque tone, she would have thought that he was making fun of her, but he wasn't. He was angry that she had once again criticized him about something so small as crumbs on the counter. She was beginning to see what a pain in the behind she was. She started to reply, but instead, grabbed her bowl of grapes and rushed out of the room. Expecting him to chase after her, she walked slower with each step and kept her eyes on the kitchen. Stopping halfway up, the disappointment of not seeing him follow her had her on the brink of tears. She waited a few more seconds and when she heard him on the phone with another one of his friends, Kyle, an old teammate, she knew she'd said a few things too much. He was getting tired of her, but not as much as she was getting tired of herself.

Seize the Moment
7

Four months into the pandemic and the impact of the virus was getting worse and worse. More of the world was still shut down and he and Aubree were still moving around each other like unfamiliar zombies. Something about her changing and he smiled every time he thought about what he was observing. From the soft kitten ways she began talking to him to the outfits she wore when he was around which kept getting tighter and smaller and with her sexy body, his imagination ran wild with a need so fierce, he was tempted on many occasions to see if she was still cold to the idea of them having sex. His hands could do so much and he was tired of self-pleasure. He wondered if she was reaching her plateau as he was.

She mentioned during one of their many fights that she was clear there would be no sex between them, but that has changed and he knew it. People often talked about human pheromones as if it were a real thing. He couldn't confirm or not confirm the validity of the idea, but he knew when Aubree was in need and her actions spoke volumes. Tonight, he was planning on testing his theory.

For the past week, she had been playing the tease and he was surprised that she wouldn't know that she knew what she was doing. She had gone from the ice princess, walking around dressed like a monk to now wearing the skimpiest scraps of material he ever saw. He was proud of how he was resisting that gorgeous body and the way he knew she could work her hips when they were in the moment. He loved how her breast fell into his hands like they were made especially for him. They were large, round, firm and the center of them would slide into his mouth like candy as he licked away at them. She had an ass that put every Kardashian to shame and even J-Lo, who he felt had the perfect body. He'd met her a time or two but still, Aubree had her beat, especially when her body stood on top of some sexy heels as she twirled around and around on the stripper pole she purchased one year for his birthday. She had done so for one night and they ended up keeping it. They both used it, though he was nowhere as good at it as she was. She took classes to perfect her craft and it showed every time she hopped on it, flipped, swung around and his favorite, slowly slid to the floor in a perfect split. Oh, how he missed those days.

What saddened him was how right she was about the past year or so when distance had grown between them. It wasn't anyone's fault and then it was also both of their fault. They had both allowed career-climbing to come between their love, taking it for granted that they would both always be there for each other. He had time to think back on things lately and she was right that he could have done better. Still, her level of anger didn't have to go as far as she took it. If he was right and she wanted back with him, she would have to do more than shake her fine ass at him and walk around showing him what he was missing by flashing her soft, creamy skin at him. He was a man made of flesh and blood but he was also a man who wanted his woman to open up to him completely and trust him. Aubree had a ways to go to do that, but he was enjoying her show. She was playing games with his affection for her and he was on to her. The question was, would she be able to handle if he rejected her like she had been rejecting him for months. Time would tell.

Of course, in the past, she never had to play any games to get him. All she had to do was look at him or touch him and that was all the invitation he would need. She was so damn beautiful and sexy as hell even if she was wearing a potato sack. Being under the same roof with her for the past few months was proving to be challenging. What shocked him the most was that they hadn't had even one argument in the past month or so and it was obvious they purposely worked on staying out of each other's way. He knew what she was planning and he would let it play out to see how far she would go.

Recently, he had to go upstairs to get some books that were in the spare bedroom where he'd put his things after removing them from the master suite. He didn't go bare feet on purpose, but he was at home and he had been relaxing on the pull-out bed in the room he was now occupying. He thought that Aubree had been asleep when he moved quietly up the stairs to not disturb her and when he reached the top step, he heard her on the phone talking to Jessica. He started to move to get what he came for when he heard Aubree explaining how she was going to try what Jessica recommended which was to use her body and her sex appeal to draw him back in. At first, he was mad that she would resort to such childishness and then he smiled, ready for her to bring it. He was ready for some excitement in their lives, but not the sexy kind; at least not yet. He wanted to see how far she would go at playing a tease.

He listened for most of their conversation, especially the part about how she was so sexually frustrated that she was ready to jump on him and demand that he ease the ache between her legs. Any other time, he would leap at the chance, never missing an opportunity to make love to her until they both collapsed from exhaustion. This wasn't going to be one of those times. Aubree had to make a change. She had to let him in and talk about what she'd been through before meeting him that wouldn't allow her to be totally free to accept his love, even with the in-your-face way he was offering it to her. They couldn't go back to the way they were, which meant they could only go forward when she was ready to leave the past, and not just their past, but the past before him, behind. They had work to do and it wouldn't be only him putting in that work if that meant he had to take extra cold showers every day when his mind began to play tricks on him with visual images of Aubree up in bed all alone, maybe touching herself or pleasuring herself in other ways that weren't him. He wanted to be there, but no more of the old way of how they worked out their issues. He had a new way in mind.

Finally finished with his last development call of the day, he wandered through the house, checking to make sure the doors were lock since both of them had gone out earlier at two different times to exercise by running around the grounds of their property since they decided to not run off-property until the virus was more under control. Feeling sure that everything was locked up for the evening, he walked into the kitchen knowing Aubree would hear him moving around and he would wage a bet that shortly, she would appear and he couldn't wait to see what she had in mind for him.

He was just about finished heating up some grilled salmon and shrimp from the day before when he heard the soft patter of Aubree's feet moving slowly down the staircase. He chuckled to himself wondering if this time, she would be bold enough to just show up naked and jump on him. There was no doubt that's what has been on her mind each time she'd shown up in yet another tempting outfit.

Two days ago, she encountered him in the laundry room where he was making enough noise for her to know he was in there and still, she acted surprised entering the room to find him emptying out the dryer. In her hands, she held a basket with five or six pieces of laundry in it to wash, something she never did because she hated wasting water, but there she was. The basket with the few items wasn't what caught his attention the most. It was Aubree coming to do laundry in a white, silk nightie that barely covered her behind and when she turned to leave after apologizing for being in his way, she somehow dropped the basket to the floor and bent all the way over to pick it up, further than she needed to, giving him a front row seat to the thin, white strip of her thong between the sexy globes of her ass, knowing exactly what she was trying to do. He didn't bite then and he wouldn't bite now. Aubree was playing a childish game and he wasn't for it. Yes, he was tempted and would like nothing more than to get between her creamy thighs with his face and his penis, but not like this. Not when he knew what was up.

As he heard her quiet footsteps moving toward the kitchen where the only light was the one over the large, rectangle marble kitchen counter, he thought back to a week ago when he was in their exercise room working out and she came in with the smallest pair of denim bootie shorts he'd ever seen. Most of her clothes he knew them when he saw them, but not those shorts. Perhaps, they had been in one of the many boxes she'd had delivered from Amazon since they were spending less and less time outdoors in stores due to the pandemic.

As he stretched on the weight bench, she apologized for interrupting his workout and that she only wanted to put extra towels in the closet in the exercise room so that they had towels on hand without having to go to the linen room on either level to get what they needed.

With the shorts, she wore one of those Daisy Duke tops that tied right under her breasts which barely held her large mounds in. He knew that was on purpose, but he closed his eyes and tried not to look in her direction. He wouldn't be enticed like that and yet, here she was again. He wondered what magnificent little number she would have on tonight.

He heard her as she entered the kitchen as he continued to clean up to head back to his room.

"Oh, I'm sorry. I hope I didn't startle you," Aubree said.

Russell smiled to himself, happy she couldn't see his face with his back to her.

"Nope, I'm not startled. Just heating up some food after a long day of work," he said.

"In the dark? Great minds must think alike. I got a little hungry too and was planning on popping a few pieces of salmon in the air-fryer while I make a small salad."

"Sounds like a plan. I'll be out of your way in a second. Just have to clean up."

Perfume. He could smell it wafting across his nose when she walked behind him toward as he inwardly chuckled to himself that she had upped her game tonight by putting on his favorite scent, Pleasures, by Estee Lauder. He had to give it to her, she was going all-in and if he turned to look at her, he knew he'd find a sexy kitten, ready to purr.

When she clicked on more light, he knew she wanted him to see her clearly and as expected, his eyes landed on taunting perfection. She was in a hot pink short satin nightie, like the white one a few nights ago. This time, the nightie was sheer on the sides, allowing him to see that she didn't have any panties on this time, not even a thong. She was completely naked underneath. Her long hair wasn't pulled up into a bun, her go-to hair style when she was home to keep it out of her face. This time, it was down, flowing around her shoulders with slight curls as if she'd just come from the salon. He knew she loved wearing sexy outfits in bed, but she hadn't done that in a long time, months before they had even broken up. Her preferred attire was one of his t-shirts, which came down over her knees. He shook his head at her as she tapped her long fingernails on the outside of the stainless-steel refrigerator, faking like she couldn't find what she was looking for.

"No need to leave on my account and I can clean that up if you want me to since I'm in the kitchen."

"Oh? Nah, don't worry about it. I know how much you hate when I leave stuff laying around. You smell nice. Is that my favorite, Pleasures?" he asked, unable to resist poking the bear. He could play games too.

"Um, yeah, I think it is. I took a hot shower a few minutes ago and felt like putting some on. It's crazy how things change in a pandemic. Who knew something as small as being able to go out of the house to places where I would normally put on perfume? I haven't done that since everything shut down. I miss so many things; I mean so, so many things. What about you? What do you miss the most?" Aubree asked.

Grabbing everything from the counter, he reached around her, making sure to rub up against her behind where she stood blocking his way. Two can play at this just as good as one could.

Placing everything on the top shelf, he didn't immediately move away. He instead, leaned close to her ear and breathed heavy for no reason. He just wanted her to know that he knew and that he would not give her the satisfaction of goading him into her web of deceit.

"I miss everything, especially your intoxicating scent and not just the perfume. Your body's natural scent drives me wild with a need so strong that it makes me drawn to you like a moth to a flame. I'd suffer getting burned just to be near you. Can you imagine wanting someone that much that you would suffer being burned by fire just to douse the desire growing inside of you?"

Adding insult to injury, he walked toward her, close, but not making contact and made kissing sounds near her ear, but did not touch her. He moaned when her essence grazed his nostrils and then did it again for good measure. He knew what sounds and actions aroused her and he already knew it was working. She may not have realized it, but he could see her shivering from his closeness. He even saw her eyes close, knowing that was when she was turned on the most. She often told him that she enjoyed closing her eyes and letting her body feel without seeing. When she exhaled as if she couldn't resist him anymore, he stepped back and smiled, waiting to see what she would say and do next. He was playing her game, but she was going to lose.

"Maybe we could..."

He waited and she said nothing else. He leaned over her before reaching around her to the counter to pick up his plate from the counter making sure he got close to her again and made a play of inhaling and adding another moan, just because.

"We could, what?" he asked near her ear.

"I..I..don't know. I was thinking..."

Again, she stopped and he could see the pulse in her neck quicken. She was ready to do anything to including go along with him if he picked her up, sat her up on the counter and planted his head between her legs, something he loved doing, but not tonight he wouldn't. He stood straight up, fixed his composure and spoke pointedly.

"You're playing Aubree, and I don't like games. Do you think I don't know what you've been trying to do? What was your end game? You thought you would do all of this wearing hot sexy outfits and no panties like tonight and I would what? Beg and plead for you to give me some? Is that where we are now?"

When she moved away from him, he knew he'd hit it on the head and she knew too.

"I'm not doing anything like that. You know I love lingerie and I didn't know you would be here in the kitchen," she uttered.

"Deny all you want. I know you could hear me because I made extra noise on purpose. You walked into the laundry room looking like a sex kitten and you suddenly appeared with the need to bring in clean towels looking like a cowgirl ready to ride. This is me you're dealing with. You think I can't smell when you're aroused?"

"What? No, I'm not."

She was stumbling over her words and with the tables turned, he was going to turn up the heat. Moving toward her again, she had no place to go with her back against the counter. He placed his hands on either side of her and leaned down so that they were face to face. What he couldn't see until now was that she also added a shiny lip gloss to her lips and a little eyeshadow to match the nightie she had on. Her naturally long lashes batted as if she had no control. He allowed his eyes to take in everything about her and he was saddened that she felt she had to play these kinds of games to get his attention. There was a time when she if she needed loving, she was the aggressor. When she wanted him to come for her, she only had to wink and he knew. This, whatever it was she was trying to do was her way of trying to get him to come back begging since they were alone and could use each other for pleasure. The thought had crossed his mind, but she'd thrown him out of their bed. The ball was in her court to lay out what she wanted. She needed to say it and come for it; not play games to make him crazy with desire for her.

"Aubree, it's as if you just met me today. We are on borrowed time. Do you understand that? I don't want to play games unless we're playing sexy games and you know how much I love those, but not this way. We have big problems that cannot be solved by me sinking deep into your body, giving you everything you and I both need. Games with our hearts or in order to manipulate each other, I don't want that. I do want you. I always have and I always will. You have a jealous streak that is out of this world and it's wrong. There are no reasons for you to be jealous. Women will flirt and you should be flattered that you have me and they can only admire from a distance. You should know who I am; the kind of man I am and I would never, ever disrespect you by having any kind of interest in another woman that isn't business or friendship. There is nothing any other woman can give to me that I can't get in my relationship with you. I understand you have issues with men because of your past and I would love to know more about that and help you get rid of those old thoughts once and for all and when you compare, you will see that I'm nothing like them. I know you and you know me. You know I love you in sexy ass lingerie like this and little, tiny shorts that show off that big, plump ass of yours and then you add my favorite perfume of yours to the mix and you say, you're not doing something? I don't like mind games. You have a need and you have too much pride now, with me, to say what that is? I'm not talking about sex; I'm talking about really talking to me and letting me in. Until you are ready to do that, we can't have anything, not even this. You feel the need to resort to enticing me after throwing me out of our bed? If it wasn't for this pandemic, we wouldn't be in the same house and then what?"

When she huffed and moved out of his embrace, he waited. She was breathing faster out of frustration that he'd caught on and not fallen victim to her womanly play.

"I don't know what you're talking about. I'm not doing anything."

"Okay, we're going to keep playing this game. Miss Kitty is lonely, I take it? You, what? You want me vulnerable, unable to resist stripping you naked and sliding inside of you to ease the ache? I know your look and reactions. I know you, baby and I also know that I don't like that you think you have to resort to this."

"I..I..I'm not lonely," she uttered.

Russell again leaned toward her ear.

"I didn't say you – I said Miss Kitty is lonely or are there extra batteries in all of those Amazon orders you've been getting lately? Look, I'm not doing this with you. If you want me, say so. If you need me, I'm right here in this house with you. You don't have to try and lure me in because none of those toys you have upstairs can do for you what I can and you know it. Trust me, there will never be enough batteries. You ended what we had for a mistake I made as if I can't make mistakes, but I was still here and I was still loving you and making a life for us, but that wasn't enough for you. I don't want to play on your insecurities that you've had when it comes to men before I met you; that wouldn't be fair and I wouldn't put you on the spot like that, but I will not stand here and let you skirt around the real issue which is you made a mistake when you made a rash decision to end our relationship. You thought I would beg you to not leave me like I've done so many times before with a promise to do better. I did nothing to warrant this and if you've had a change of heart and want to really deal with us, you let me know. If all you want is for me to satisfy you, no more games. Just say it. I want you. I will always want you. That will never, ever change, but this is not a game and we are not teenagers. I love you and if being in the midst of a pandemic where people are losing their lives to this virus hasn't made you take stock in what we had and appreciate it, then that's on you. When you are ready to really, really talk to me, let me know and I'll be all ears. I will listen to anything you want to share, but you have to be ready to share it all. I'm talking everything that's holding you back from loving me unconditionally because that's how I love you."

Aubree's head lowered and he knew he touched a nerve.

"I don't know how to do that. I'm not like you. I have bad memories of relationships."

"Baby, you think I don't know that? I know of a few, but there is more going on and it's keeping you from me. It's keeping you from loving me. It's keeping you from accepting what is real, true love. That has to be hard, but until you're ready to lean on me and trust me with your heart and your stories, I can't do this with you. I want you. I want you so much, but not like this. You can run freezing cold one second and when you're in heat, you're hot like fire and ready to spread eagle for me. There is nothing wrong with that, but there is something wrong with how you ended us. I'm ready to talk about what keeps you from me fully when you're ready."

"It's just sex, Russell."

"No, baby, it's life. It's my life, your life and our life together. I love sex, you know that and I don't want it with anyone but you, but it's not a fix to us; talking is."

"I don't know what to do," she lamented.

He was feeling sorry that she was so torn, but this was a hard pill he needed her to swallow, but also needed her to know that she was still the most desirable woman he'd ever met.

"Take some time and think about what I said. Now, to bring my point home..."

Russell cut his words off and kept his eyes locked on hers as he reached up to caress her face as he ran his finger across the sheen on her lips. He could see her breaths increasing with every pass of his fingers across her lips.

Letting his finger glide across the seam of her lips, no words were spoken as he encouraged her lips open. The moment she did, he slipped his finger inside, moving it around her tongue and then pulled it out again. With his lips mere inches from hers, he reached down, moving his hand slowly up her thigh to that place he missed and loved so much. Finding what he was searching for, he smiled when Aubree held her breath the moment his finger came in contact with her womanhood.

"Moist and slippery when wet," he whispered against her lips. "Sheen on both sets of your lips and I love it."

Taking his hand, he slipped his finger into his own mouth, slowly licking her essence from is and watched her desire-filled, hooded eyes, full with unadulterated lust as they followed the actions of his tongue.

"Um," Aubree uttered.

"You want me to taste you, love you, have you screaming to the rafters, you can have it whenever you want it, but stop playing games with me. You and I both deserve better than that. I love you, Aubree, and I don't want to be some guy who services you because you're horny. I want to still be your man who fills all of your needs. I'm not perfect and neither are you and if you come to me, it's because you want to work things out or at least try to. It won't be this because you have a strong stiff one living in the same house as you."

Turning and leaving her standing in a heightened state of arousal that he never remembered seeing before in all of the years they'd been together, he took his plate and left the kitchen, leaving his love standing their contemplating her next move. He hoped she would choose them.

Seize the Moment
8

Two nights. That's how long it took for her to face Russell after he peeped her game in the kitchen the other night. She did what he asked and she thought about all that he'd said. She weighed her life without him to her life with him and she knew that she didn't want to be without him. Truth was, no man had ever handled her with such care as he had, knowing she had trust issues with men. He knew it and he still loved her. He tolerated her many mood swings and loved her anyhow. He never gave up on her until she finally gave up on him in a big way. She lived with that every day that she went to bed alone with him in the same house in a different room. The idea of that was still foolish to her.

She had time to think back over their relationship over the years and a lot of points of contention were due to her lack of trust in him based on her lack of trust of men in general. Russell wasn't to blame for that. If she were really truthful with herself, if anyone could help her overcome her hurt, it was him, the one man who has never hurt her at all. She's never been able to find any proof of infidelity and she was angry at herself that she would look for it. Was she really going to be petty and blame him for things he's never done to her?

The day was leading into night and she'd finally gotten up the nerve to try and be this open and transparent person that he wanted and needed her to be. She often marveled at how easily he expressed himself with her, telling her some of his deepest, darkest secrets. She skated around telling him everything about her, some things too painful to tell anyone, but with Russell, she was ready to try because she wanted his love and trust back. She needed him to know that she will never, ever do this to them again. Every day she thanked her lucky stars that despite breaking up, they were still living in the same house and she hadn't run out of time to make things right.

Two nights ago, he left the door open for her to come to him if and when she was ready. She could tell that his words meant never again would he allow her to put aside her behavior and act as if there weren't any problems. She would only get to the root of them by letting go with him; by searching her past and bringing it to the table so that he could help her get over them. For so many years, she kept secrets, afraid that telling anyone would them judging her, but not Russell. Deep down, she knew he wouldn't do that.

That's why, she was now on her way down the steps in the pitch-black house. The only light came from the bright moon outside that lit her path as she walked. It had been a few hours since she had last heard Russell moving around and she wondered if now that she'd gotten up the nerve to go talk to him, she would find him fast asleep, missing the chance to keep her guard down.

As she walked up to his room where the door was wide open, she was surprised to find he wasn't watching television or listening to music, though it was only eight in the evening. Usually, he kept late hours due to recording of his hit talk show, but tonight, he seemed to be asleep. She thought about turning around, but instead, went further into the room. She could see the outline of his body and the moon outside of the four large floor to ceiling windows allowed her to see that he was laying on his back with one leg on top of the blanket with the other underneath. He didn't have on a shirt, just what looked like boxer briefs. She knew he usually slept in the nude, but these days, he seemed to have done away with that.

Moving closer to the bed, she looked over at him and didn't say a word. She struggled with whether to stay or leave. The decision was made for her.

"Are you going to stand there and stare or did you plan to say something since you crept all the way down here? And yes, I could hear you moving around and heading in this direction."

Aubree wrangled her hands nervously.

"Oh, you're awake. You were so still I thought you were sleeping. I was surprised the television wasn't on watching you the way you like."

She still hadn't entered the room fully, but stood in the doorway and leaned over to get a better look at him. She didn't know whether to stay or leave. All the nerve she had in her bedroom which had her up and creeping around the house was suddenly slipping away now that she was here, in his room, with him awake. When the room was quickly illuminated with light from the lamp next to the sofa that turned into a bed, she moved a little further into the room.

"Sort of between being asleep and being awake. I'm exhausted, but I'm not recording for a few days since it's the weekend, so I'm good."

"Am I disturbing you? I didn't want to do that."

Idle chatter was not her thing and her attempt at it sounded weird.

"What is it, Aubree? You're here now. I haven't seen you in a couple of days. Imagine that, considering neither of us have really left the house."

He's still angry, she thought. She didn't blame him because he'd called her out for exactly what she had been doing and she was embarrassed; even around him.

"I know. I've been doing some thinking and I was hoping we could talk."

She could see his face and he wasn't smiling or showing even a hint that he was happy to see her, but she was hoping to change that. When Russell's eyes traveled her body from her head where her long hair was pulled up into a high ponytail to down her body which was covered in a two piece, long-sleeved red and black flannel-like pajama set to her feet encased in Betty-Boop socks, she wondered if her blatant attempt to prove she wasn't trying to get him into bed was obvious. The appearance of a crooked smile on his handsome face provided her answer.

"Really? You go from tiny shorts to full armor in flannel?" he laughed.

Aubree tried not to laugh, but couldn't help herself. She felt silly. The socks were her staple favorite, but the pajamas were a bit much. They had been a Christmas gift from her mother a few years ago and this was her first time wearing them.

"I know. I'm all over the place, right? That's kind of what I wanted to talk to you about."

"Well, since you're in flannel, I guess it's okay for you to sit here on the bed."

She watched him swing his legs out from under the think black and white striped blanket and noticed his only clothing was a pair of black boxer briefs. She tried to focus on the task at hand of talking to him, but her mind went to the many days and nights she'd spent under and on top of those muscled thighs. Not only was it the best love making she'd ever had in her life, but in his arms and wrapped around his body, she felt loved. She needed to focus and looked to his face and not the bare chest that she was itching to kiss and caress.

"I didn't want you to think I was trying to play any games and you were right, I was. I really do want to talk and just talk. You said come to you when I was ready and I want to try."

For several seconds, neither of them said a word. She tried not to look his way afraid that even in the dark, she wouldn't find compassion in his eyes knowing that they had been more estranged lately than ever, though they've had issues over the years. A deep look into herself and what she brought to the times of disparage in their relationship, she discovered the root of most of their drama was her and she was ready to admit that. The problem was, she didn't know how Russell would receive it and if he would see that she was speaking from a new place within her heart and not the place of just wanting them to get back together. It was bigger than that; much bigger.

"Aubree?"

Hearing her name brought her out of her cone of silence and she knew now was the time.

"I'm sorry, Russell. I'm sorry that I got us here. I didn't mean for things to go this far. We've had disagreements before, but nothing that tore us apart like we are now. I'm sorry we're here," she mumbled out, suddenly feeling like she was going to cry. She'd done enough of that into the pillows on her bed in hopes that she could get it out without him hearing her. She didn't want to cry now – not in front of Russell. She wanted his love and understanding, but not his pity or sympathy.

"How did we get here? What's really going on? Are you really ready to talk to me? Because, see, in the past, we've had arguments and what we have always done was to make it go away by sweating it out between the sheets. In truth, that never solves anything, it only puts a band-aid over a problem that we never really resolve. What happened Valentine's night ended us. You actually ended us out of anger without really talking to me, instead talking at me."

"I know and being totally transparent here, I thought you would eventually come to bed and we'd make up, but you didn't. You gave up."

"Aubree, you told me you were through with me. You didn't want me in our bed or in this house we live in and made a home together. Do you not remember that night and how angry you were over nothing? It really was nothing, but I'll give you the benefit of the doubt that it was something to you. I got that, but you dismissed me like I was some random guy and that was crushing. How was I supposed to come to bed with you after that?"

"I didn't mean it."

"You never do, but that night was different and I didn't have the fight in me. Do you know that if it were not for this pandemic, I would be gone? We wouldn't be seeing each other or possibly not even talking to each other? I was going to give you what you wanted and then the world went to hell with this virus."

"I know and the weight of that hit me a few hours ago. After all this time, a few hours ago, realized I could lose you for good and I don't want that; I never wanted that."

"Why, Aubree? Why do we keep ending up here? What am I doing wrong? I try to love you, support you, be there for you, give you want you want and what you need and still I'm the bad guy. It's been a few years of this back and forth and I can't keep up. What's the real issue here? If you want to really talk, let's do that. We never do that. We never really talk. We argue, screw like rabbits and then after that, all is forgiven without anything being addressed because that's how you want it. You use sex to get back to normal and I've always obliged you, but I can't do that anymore. Explain to me what's really going on with you?"

"I still have insecurity issues and sex with us, when we were actually having it on the regular, was my way of getting on the better side of my issues with not feeling worthy or knowing if I'm really wanted."

"What? I have never made you feel like you're unworthy or not wanted. Actually, let me say that better. If I have ever done that, I didn't know I was doing that and I apologize if that's the case. I love you more than anything in this world, but I have found that no matter how many times I say or show that, you find a reason to question it."

"I know and it's not you."

"Okay, then talk to me," Russell said.

Aubree searched her thoughts and after years of never being able to be completely honest, she was ready because she needed and wanted to fight for them. Her old ways of repairing issues between them didn't work this time and she knew if she didn't come clean, she would lose him for good.

"Do you remember how we met?" she asked as her eyes searched his face.

"I do. You were dating David Butler, the number two star basketball center on the team that was the staunchest competitors to my team. He hated me because he couldn't knock me off that throne at the top spot. That was some rivalry. He thought he was better because he was younger, but that never showed on the court. I know that was a bad situation for you and I knew what you'd gone through. I knew of his reputation and so did everyone else in the league. I remember one night when I was at my condo in Chicago, I couldn't sleep with a big game coming up and it was on my home turf, so I had to bring that win home. I get up and head to this all-night diner for my favorite comfort food, pancakes and in the back corner of the diner in a booth all by yourself was you. I didn't see you as soon as I walked in, but at one time, I thought I could hear you crying and when I looked your way, you were wiping away tears. I saw a beautiful woman sitting alone and crying and I couldn't ignore that. I walked over to ask if you were okay, if you felt safe or if something was going on that I could help with, like if you were in a situation at the moment that could cause you harm and when you finally said you were fine, just getting through an emotional relationship rollercoaster. I remember I cracked a corny joke to make you laugh and when you did, I felt better that no one was there harming you. Since no one ever joined you, we talked until you said it was okay for me to sit down at your table because looking up at me was giving you a pain in your neck. We talked until the sun came up and then I waited with you until your cab came and I thought that was it."

"Wow, you still have a vivid recollection five years later?" she asked. This was the first time in a very long time that they'd talked about that night. To her, it was a night she'd never forget for more reasons than one, both good and bad.

"I do. It was the night I met the love of my life and I would never forget it, not even one detail. I also remember you had on a black sweatsuit and your hair was cut short with sexy blond highlights. I remember you were in strappy heels with your feet out, really high ones and it was freezing outside. I didn't get why you would come out in Chicago weather when it had snowed the night before."

"Oh, yeah, the heels. My feet were pretty frozen by the time I got back to my hotel room. That night, before you came along, had been a night like so many others I had experienced. My relationships with men had always turned volatile and that year with David was the worst. He shattered my self-esteem and any trust I had in relationships was crushed. I don't know what I was thinking staying with him for so long knowing he openly cheated on me regularly and then to leave me in that diner alone was a shock to my system."

"It wasn't until after we started dating that you told me about him leaving you at the diner that night, in the middle of the night to get back to your hotel the best way you could.

When I saw you at the game a few nights later sitting with the team wives and girlfriends behind him, I didn't think anything of it until cameras caught up to him after the game where his team lost. I watched the news footage again and again when at first, you were walking hand-in-hand to his car outside of a club and he started shouting at you to walk faster and some other choice words I won't repeat. And then it happened. I watched him get in the driver's side and speed off without even unlocking the door to let you in. He left you standing on the parking lot with cameras flashing in your face while you tried to hold back the tears of embarrassment of being left and dismissed like that. I wanted to pound him into the ground."

"That night was horrible. It wasn't the first time he'd done that to me and the diner abandonment wasn't the first time either."

"It took me a few days to find out more than just your first name so that I could check on you. Thankfully, though David and I didn't like each other because of the competitive nature of the game, I had a few friends on his team who told me where you were staying after he dismissed you. Was David the first guy you allowed to treat you like that?" Russell asked.

Aubree wasn't one for deep conversations into her personality and into her life, but she knew it was way beyond the time to put her heart and her thoughts on the line to salvage what she could of their relationship. She was so used to men falling at her feet because of her beauty and having Russell agree to walk away and not fight for them was her wakeup call. He'd never done that before and she was caught off-guard that he didn't come running to apologize and beg for her to forgive him. It's how men had treated her over the years and that's what she always did, beg and plead with them to not leave her.

"No, he was just the worse when it came to how he treated me. If you're going to ask me why I accepted that, I can't answer that, but I truly don't know. I guess I'm broken," she admitted and lowered her head so that he couldn't see her eyes. She, instead, focused on her hands as they nervously shook on her lap.

"Don't do that. Look at me, Aubree."

She was too embarrassed.

"I can't," she said softly.

"Baby, look at me. You can always look at me and you can always tell me anything. It's been five years and we've skated around so many issues, most I don't even remember, but I don't remember us ever sitting down and talking like this and I want to make this count. I want you to look at me and see that there is no judgement here. Not in this house, not on my face and not in my words. You have things that you have been dealing with for a long time and you've never really let me in and I've let us live on the outside of our relationship avoiding any real, deep talks and look where that got us. No more, baby. No more. Look at me," Russell declared again. "Say what you need to say. I am here. Talk to me."

Aubree let go and the words came.

"David once forced himself on me and it was horrible. The worse part of that was there was another man in the room and I didn't know it. He thought because he was a ballplayer and could get any woman he wanted, that he would do whatever he wanted with me. I was so insecure; I think searching for love when I knew I wouldn't find it with him. Since back in high school, I was always the prettiest and boys wanted me. I was popular, a cheerleader and everyone would say I was too beautiful, if that was such a thing. I just wanted to be loved after I found out that I was adopted. When my parents told me about how my biological parents deserted me, they told me all of it and then when I was able to meet them, at their request, I find out that they had more children after me, but made me feel like having me was some kind of curse. I never saw them again. Though my adoptive parents loved me and never treated me any different than my sister and brother that they gave birth to, I still had a desire to love the parents who didn't want me. Meeting me at, ten or eleven, they made it clear that they were happy they met me and that I had a good life, but they didn't want any further communication with me after asking to meet me. I turned rejection that into getting in relationships with men who didn't really love me, but I thought I could make them love me because I was pretty. Anyway, one night, David told me he wanted to do something different. He bought me this sexy black lace two-piece lingerie set along with a garter belt and blindfold. He wanted to see me in it and I obliged. He had a game in Miami I think is where we were because he owned a condo there. This was before I met you, so yes, if you're thinking it, this happened and I stayed with him."

"No judgment baby. Just let it out and we can handle whatever it is. Of course, right now, I want to kill him without even hearing the whole story, but this moment is about you and not him. I'm listening."

She tried to turn her face away, but he wasn't having any of that. She felt his hands on her chin as he slowly turned her head back around to face him and when their eyes locked, she saw a safe place for her feelings and her story.

"He took a hot bath, put on makeup, the lingerie he bought and these high, high heels. He had been waiting for me to come out and when I did, he kept giving me compliments on top of compliments and asking me to spin around and twirl and just do whatever he wanted me to do. I thought we were in for a nice quiet night together to make up for all the things he done to me like cheating and cursing me out, just because. Eventually, he took me by the hand and we went into the bedroom. Are you sure you want to hear all of this?" she asked.

"I want to hear anything you want to tell me. Keep your hands in mine and feel my touch. I'm here with you," Russell said; his words easing the tension in her body.

"In the bedroom, we were in the bed doing things and I heard this noise. He was on top of me and behind him I saw a red light. I knew immediately what it was. There was someone in the closet recording us. I tried to struggle once I knew what was happening and he pinned me down, calling to his buddy in the closet to come out and get a close up. I fought and struggled and with his hand over my mouth and his friend taping and both of them laughing, he forced himself on me against my struggles. It seemed to go on forever. When he was done, he said this was the kind of something new he wanted from me because he felt like I was too stuck up. I was his woman and I should do what he asked to please him. He didn't see what that moment did to me and I was too embarrassed to move. I pulled a blanket over myself and just laid there while they drank, smoked and watched what his friend taped. He claimed I was special because he would never trust a friend to record us and watch us. When they both passed out drunk, I got out of there and called my adoptive sister who paid for me to take a plane back home. My family was living in Fort Worth, Texas at that time. I was wild back then. Really out of control, thinking I was something because I had a ballplayer. I didn't want the next girl to have him and so I went home and avoided him for a few days until he left a message that I had better meet him in Washington, D.C. for his next game. He expected to see me sitting with the wives and girlfriends and that I better get over being so skittish about sex."

"Wait, does David have a video of you?" Russell asked her. She could hear the tension in his voice that depending on how she answered, he would decide what his next move would be. She alleviated his concern immediately.

"No. When they passed out, I took the handheld video camera. It was one of those small, JVC kind that once you recorded, you needed to plug it into a computer in order to share it in any way. I took it when I slipped out and when I got to the airport, I saw a flower bed with a bunch of large rocks. I picked up one, took the camera to a corner of the garage and destroyed it into little pieces. I dropped pieces of it in various trashcans, feeling good that I got rid of it. He was mad that I did that, but the season was heating up and he quickly forgot and clearly, so did I. We moved beyond that like it never happened. I couldn't tell anyone. I was too afraid of what would happen if I did. My family would know, friends and I thought that he would tell everyone, making it sound like I wanted that. I let it go, but not really. I never trusted anyone fully again and because of that, I couldn't love you like you want and need."

111

"Baby, you can. I don't hold anything against you and despite what you told me and what we've been through, I love you so much. Nothing about you could ever change that; nothing. For the first time, you shared something so personal and I thank you for doing that. Do you trust that I would never share that with anyone? Do you trust that I love you so much that your past doesn't matter to me? I hope you trust me enough to help you deal with everything in your past in whatever way you want. If you want to talk to someone or just talk to me, I'm here for it all. That was a horrible thing that jackass did to you and I can't say I won't try to hurt him if I run across him again. I doubt if that will happen because after he was thrown out of the league, he wasted all of his money and I hear, he had gone to Mexico and came across the wrong guys who beat him up pretty bad for something he did to a woman. It's the talk through the league, but I don't how factual it is. I want to focus on you and what your needs are. That's all that matters. Working on you is all that matters."

"What can I do to fix us? I mean, I know where we are is my fault, but I don't want this and I know if it wasn't for the pandemic, we may not even be talking and that would have destroyed me and I would have let it because pride would have kept me from coming to you like this, open and vulnerable. I don't want this. I don't want us apart."

"Pride is a dangerous thing and it never amounts to anything good. Tell me what you're really feeling about us. Tell me why you never seem to trust me though I have never given you any reason to question my commitment and dedication to you. Since the very second we started seeing each other, I may look at women, but I'm a man and I'm going to look, but not once have I ever considered stepping out on you; not once. You have always been enough for me. I work hard to make sure we can live comfortably. I support everything you want to do in life and in your career. I even put up with your father who we both know would suck us dry if we let him, but because you love him in spite of how he treats you, I tolerate him because I love you. I love you, I desire you, I cherish you, but I admit, I'm not perfect and I do mess up when I forget things, but the way you spoke to me Valentine's night was far out of what I could tolerate. I tried to apologize and for the week or so after that night, you went in on me which is why I originally decided to juts move into a temporary situation until I found something more permanent. Things had gotten pretty crazy. I understand your frustration and I'm still sorry for not making more of that day. I swear, I thought you would understand knowing the kind of pressure I was under for the show."

Hearing him lay out how sorry he was made her feel even worse. She knew she'd gone overboard, but she got angrier when day after day went by and he didn't approach her to apologize the way they usually did. She overacted that night, something she discovered right away, but it was too late to pull back how she acted and what she said.

"No, don't. I know you've apologized several times for that night and I was just crazy with jealousy thinking that all of your time couldn't be spent working on your show. I thought you were seeing other women. I was talking to Jessica, Melanie and Toya and I let Toya get in my head that you were cheating on me and that's all I could think about every time you came home late. I went there without even talking to you and I knew I shouldn't have done that."

"Wait – you let those women convince you that your man, the one you live with and know better than any of the, that I was out here messing around on you and you went with that? You didn't think to approach me without accusing me. You went straight to I'm guilty because Toya said so? You know my thoughts about single women who can keep a man dishing out ideology like they know what's best for everyone else's relationships while she changes men as often as she changes hair. Was Jessica telling you that too? That's my girl and you know it. She always has your back and I would consider her a real friend to you. She said that too? She did that to you?"

"No, she didn't. In fact, she shut Toya down, from what I'm told. After I told her what Toya said, she gave me forty lashes for even going there with no proof. I let my mind go there because of past relationships."

"Baby, I'm not one of those relationships with trashy, disrespectful men you've had. I've always shown you nothing but the utmost respect. As far as Toya goes, you need to check our girl. Did Jessica tell you she tried to come at me about a year ago?"

Aubree's back shifted to an upright position as she whipped her entire body around to face him.

"Toya did what? What are you talking about?"

"Okay, I never want to come between you and your girls. I'm not that guy that points out their faults to try and have you friendless, but Toya is just as foul as you once told me she was with other men. I had gone out the last night of me sitting in for the biggest late night show host who topped the charts before I came along. Some of the fellas and I decided to go out and celebrate. This was when you had gone to visit with your mother for her surgery. You were gone for like two weeks to Atlanta. Toya came on strong, making a play for me. I had gone over to the bar to grab a drink since our waitress was taking so long. Toya came up to me being all playful and coy and then talked about how lonely I must be with you gone and actually came out and asked how she could help me while you were gone and we could keep it to ourselves and that no one had to know. I was letting her know it would never happen and in the next second, just as I was about to call her out of her name, Jessica arrived on the scene like the Black Widow and snatched Toya by her hair, pulling her away.

Jessica came back later and I thought that she didn't hear the whole conversation to know that I was never entertaining anything with Toya. Instead, she said she heard it all and was thankful that I would never disrespect you that way. A few days later, she said that she talked to Toya who begged her not to tell you because it was the alcohol that had her behaving that way. Jess didn't want to hurt you and so she said she wanted it to just go way, but from that day on, I always kept Toya at arm's length. She wasn't around much after that and I was fine with that."

"Now, I know why she prefers to text or talk on the phone, but never hang out and she hasn't been here to the house in a year, no matter how many ladies nights out I invited her to. She's always been jealous of me being with you and I knew it, but I never thought she'd go behind my back and make a play for you."

"Jess had your back, trust me. I was afraid of Jess after that. The way she snatched Toya up was frightening," he laughed.

"Jess is my friend and you are the love of my life. I know you love me."

"I'm understanding why you're so reserved and it's okay. You can work on that and I can help you if you'll let me."

Aubree nodded, overwhelmed with too much emotion to speak on it.

"I know I need to see someone professional to talk through my problems and I want to do that. I think it would help me understand a lot about myself and how I can deal with trust issues."

"You've gone through a lot and now I have a better understanding, something I didn't have before. I'm here for you. You know, we've never talked like this. I mean, I can't remember a time where we've really talked to get to the root of the problem. I'm not saying that I haven't had my part in our problems, but I knew you had deep issues with men that kept you from giving yourself fully to loving our love. I know that took a lot out of you to tell me that and I'm thankful you trust me enough to share. I am here if and when you want to talk if it will help."

"This helped a lot. I think I need to walk this off a bit."

"Outside this time of night? No, not even on the property."

"I'm thinking about hitting the treadmill to walk it off.

Aubree stood and walked toward the door, moving with slow steps hoping Russell would stop her before she left the room. He didn't and that made her sad. With her back to him, she had to say a few last words.

"Could we survive what I put us through? Is there any chance that we could get to a better place and not give up on each other or at least, can you not give up on me? I know I'm asking a lot and that I've been a lot to deal with. My moods have been all over the place and my trust issues keep getting in the way, but can you tell me if I've lost you for good? Before you answer, let me be as transparent as possible. I was talking with Jess and I was desperate. I never thought you'd actually leave me and I was wrong for that because that was playing with both of our emotions, trying to get you to conform and that was wrong. I put out the challenge and you didn't respond the way I thought and that was my loss. I asked her to help me get you back and not like in the past when we would get over stuff quick without talking. Tonight, talking to you made me feel better than I've felt in a long time and I love you. She meant well with her advice of playing the tease, using what I've got to get what I want, were her exact words. I was willing to try that and then after you talked to me last night in the kitchen, I realized what I was doing was wrong. I was trying to use sex to reign in control of our relationship and I'm ashamed. When the pandemic is over and we can get back to our lives, are you through with me?"

Never had she been this open and vulnerable with a man. In her past, she had allowed men to treat her any kind of way just to keep him. She was always attracted to men who never wanted just one woman until she met Russell and she couldn't believe he actually wanted her. For five years, she'd been waiting for the brick to fall and he would turn out to be just like all the rest, but he wasn't the problem; she was.

"Are saying this and asking because you want to get back to where we were as if it didn't happen because I can't do that. I can't be the punching bag for everything other men have done to you. I've been here and I've tried to show you that you matter, that you're loved, but you push me away and when you push, you push hard. I've tried to get you to open up to me so that you can feel safe to let your guard down. Tonight was different and I'm glad our talk helped you feel better and it's helped me understand that part of you that you've been holding back from me. I can't say what will happen after the pandemic, but we are here, now, together until who knows when and because of that, we can work on it. I don't want to give up on us and definitely not on you. I told you I've never told a woman I loved her before that wasn't my mother or my sister. I meant it that day and I've meant it ever since. What about you?" he asked.

She turned around and faced him, no longer running away or shying away from putting her heart on the line.

"I love you and I'm sorry for being childish. For five years, I've been afraid of losing you to another woman and I guess each time I thought it was happening, I made a play to get out first before you hurt me."

"Come here."

Walking back over to the bed, she entered the space between his legs and placed her hands on his shoulders as he placed his hands on her hips.

"Don't pacify me; be honest," she said.

"I don't think I could ever not love you. One thing this pandemic will allow us to do is really spend time together that we've been missing for at least a year due to our schedules because where are we going to go. This thing with the virus doesn't appear to be slowing down. I want to try and work on us, keep talking and sharing and getting deep into what we need to do to fix us and how I can help you get over your past to know that your present and your future with me would be nothing like back then. Baby, I'm not that kind of man."

"I know you're not; I really do know that now. I want to try."

When Russell yawned, she realized how late the hour was and after a busy day of taping his show, he had to be exhausted.

"I'm down for that, too. We'll take it slow."

"You're tired," she said, rubbing his temples, smiling when he laid his head on her stomach as she massaged his head the way he loved when he needed to relax. "I'm going to go to bed so that you can get some sleep."

When she tried to pull away, Russell's arms went around her waist, holding her tight to him.

"I miss you," he uttered against her.

"I miss you, too."

"Stay with me. No sex, just stay with me; here, the rest of the night. Do you know how hard it's been not being close to you?"

"I know it's been killing me, too. When we're good, we're really good and I miss that. There's so much I've been taking for granted and every time I see the news and hear about another person dying from this virus, another family left wondering if they will lose someone, I think about how precious life and love are."

Russell yawned again and she smiled as she held him tighter. When his head started to droop and his arms kept dropping and then gripping her again, she knew he was falling asleep.

"I miss you so much, baby."

"I know, but you also miss sleep which I know you haven't gotten much of this past week. Lay down," she demanded.

"You're going to say?" he asked.

"Of course, but no more talking."

"Can we sleep in late? I'm talking about most of the day tomorrow. I've been so busy, you've been busy and we haven't lain in bed together in a long time without rushing to get out of it to get to someplace else. I'm off for the next two days and nights."

"Yes. I'm going to take a few days off so that we can focus on us like never before."

Another big yawn from Russell had her pushing him back onto the bed and covering him with the lightweight comforter that covered the bed. After turning off the bedside lamp and walking around to the other side of the bed, the light from the bright moon outside of the window shown on his face and she could see that he was already asleep. He looked so peaceful and so tired. How could she ever question a man who was as dedicated to her and to their life as he was. She had to work on herself so that she wouldn't lose the best man that ever happened to her.

Pulling back the comforter, she slid under it and the moment he felt her near, he pulled her snug against his body, kissed her sweetly on the lips and just that fast, he was sound asleep with his arms holding her tight. Moving as close to him as she could, she caressed his face, his lips and then his cheek and then closed her own eyes. She never wanted to have a life that didn't have him in it.

Seize the Moment
9

Russell could feel Aubree moving around in his arms and he wasn't sure if she was trying to get comfortable or slip out of bed. He didn't know how long he'd been asleep, but he was now woke and happy knowing that having her in his arms wasn't a dream.

"You're moving. Are you leaving?" he murmured against her ear.

"No, I'm not leaving and you should be asleep. I was feeling around for the remote to the blinds to close them. When daylight comes up, I didn't want the sun to wake you up."

"It's not over there. I think it's under the bed. I dropped it and never picked it up. You can't sleep?" he asked.

When Aubree turned and faced him, he pulled her closer, thankful for the light from the moon so that he could see some of her.

"I was dreaming and it woke me up, but I'm comfortable enough to go back to sleep."

"What were you dreaming about?" he asked.

"Us."

"Us? What about us?"

When silence lived after his question, he hoped she wasn't reverting back to her shell of not knowing how to really express her feelings. He wanted to move forward, not backward.

"We were making love."

"Ah. In your dream? Was it hot?"

"Steamy, burning hot. I've had many of those about you. In fact, I had a really hot one a few days after that night we broke up."

"Mmm, I love it. Tell me what we were doing. Put me back to sleep from your dream."

"Russell!"

"Baby, I'm serious. I want to hear it. Don't get shy on me. We should be able to talk about anything. Do you know that I've always wanted to hear you tell me what turns you on? I know you have no problem showing me and I love that too, but I want you to feel comfortable saying the words. I want you to say anything you want and not feel shy or like I would think some kind of negative thoughts about you. This is me and you and no one else. Don't you love when I talk dirty to you? No need to answer because I can tell by how you react to me that it makes you feel hot and bothered and more than ready for more. Tell me. What were you dreaming about tonight?"

"Ugh, I'm in flannel and it's already hot in these pajamas."

"Take them off."

"Russell!"

He laughed out loud when he lightly punched his chest.

"You said you're hot and after you tell me about this

dream, I bet you'll be even hotter."

"You know what this will lead to and I don't want you to think I planned this because I ran out of batteries."

Her comment was unexpected and he tried to control the laugh from his gut that came out of him.

"It broke me to deny you sex when I knew you were playing with me, but I would never leave you stranded when you don't have any batteries left. You been giving them toys a workout, huh?"

"You're making fun of me?"

If she hadn't laughed after asking that, he would have asked if she was serious. This was how he wanted them to be. So much of how they should have been with each other had been lost for a long time and he was more than happy to get back to it and then some.

"Never. I got what those toys could never replace. Now, tell me about your dream while I help you get these hot ass pajamas off."

Proceeding to do exactly what he said, he reached down and slid the bottoms off and as his hand traveled up her body, his body rose to the occasion when he felt the think strap on her hip the thong she had on. From the moment she entered the room, he had been wondering what she had on underneath. He loved her in thongs, seeing that material disappear between the plump cheeks of her behind.

"In my dream, I was in the kitchen cooking."

"Wait, slow and set the scene for me. What do you have on?" he asked while unbuttoning the top to the pajamas and quickly tossing it to the floor as his excitement went to a whole new level when his hands traveled around her body even more, finding her braless taking one of her large mounds in his hand, giving it a soft squeeze.

"I had on one of those skinny strap, black satin nighties. I was at the counter doing something and you walked up behind me. You didn't say a word. Your hands were everywhere, all over my body."

Making her dream more of a reality, he let his hand roam all over her body and delighted when she moaned against his lips as they faced each other in the bed.

"Like this," he whispered on a sexual groan, getting turned on by the second.

"More."

"Mmm, more in the dream or more now?"

"Both. Ah."

Russell let his hand slip down to the area between her legs and when she parted them a little giving him better access, he took her leg and put it up on his hip, opening her for him.

"Keep going. What else? What did I do?"

"You, um, wait."

"You want me to stop?" he asked, salaciously, leaning over and licking a path across whatever part of her chest he could find in the dark. He smiled knowing what it was doing to her. They'd always had a good sex life, but not for a long time and he knew it was time to get back to it. He was seizing the moment and appreciating her for the sexy woman she was.

"No – don't stop. I lost my thought for a minute. I can't think with your hand being between my legs. Okay, um, I had a plate or something in my hand. You took it and placed my hands flat on the kitchen island and told me to leave them there. It was so hot!"

"Ah, you like that. I can tell because my fingers are coated in something wet. You liked that in your dream?"

"Yes."

"Continue, baby. What happened next?"

While she tried to find her words, he took his time sliding her thong down her legs and then put her one leg back up and across his hip, placing his hand back between her legs.

"I turned around a little and you were already naked. I was about to say something and you told me to speak, just feel."

"How are you feeling now?" he asked against her lips.

"Like I'm on fire, just like in my dream."

"Is the reality better?"

"Way better, ah. Your fingers feel amazing."

"Would you like more?"

"Yes."

"Tell me what you want."

He felt her hand slide between them and land on his hardness which was straining against the inside of his briefs. Not wanting anything to be between what she wanted and needed, he leaned up, slid them off and went back to his position.

"This," she uttered with breathy pants.

"You sure?"

"Yes."

"Show me just how much."

"I thought we weren't going to refrain from sex. You know, because of how I've tricked you in the past."

"So, you don't want to make love right now?" he asked and chuckled, already know the answer.

"Yes."

"Yes, you don't or yes you do?"

When she stroked him more aggressively with perfection, he had his answer.

He had to search for every bit of restraint he could muster up to take this night nice and slow. No rushing. No quickie. He wanted them to enjoy the moment in the still of the night with no sound other than their passionate moans.

When she caressed him, the feeling of her hand on him was different. He could see the whites of her eyes, which was also new. She usually preferred her eyes closed and he never pushed for her to open her eyes and live in the moment. Increasing the speed and the pressure of her hand, his hips bucked with a slight jerk forward. She was feeling and seeing him together at once, for the first time. They were experiencing the level of intimacy he always wanted to have with her.

"You see me," he said, saying each word between soft kisses to her lips.

"I do."

"I see you too, sweetheart."

"I'm letting go," she proclaimed. "I'm going to finally let go and take us for who we are and not let any fear get in the way. I love you, Russell."

"You're mine; I'm yours and in this moment, it's just me and you and I'm vulnerable to you, baby. I'm wide open, my love, my life, my heart – they are all intertwined with you."

"I'm ready."

No more words, Russell only wanted to love.

"Keep your eyes on me. Don't close them."

Rolling over, he moved into the space between her legs,

taking her hands and placing them above her head. Reaching for the lamp on the table beside the bed, he lit up the room in a soft glow. He wanted to be sure they saw all of each other as they made love with her eyes open.

"This moment," Aubree whispered.

The glint in her eyes told the only story he needed to know. The last vestige of a wall between them was gone.

"I'm seizing it baby, but not just for now, not just for tonight, but we're going to seize every moment and do better with making each other a priority."

To show her just how much of a priority she was, he took her lips and made love to them. He took his time with slow deliberate kisses and then suckled where he'd just kissed. He moved his lips all over her face then down her neck before settling on her ear. When her body wiggled beneath him, he knew she was enjoying his touch, his caress. Knowing they had all night to experience all levels of intimacy and he would get to that. His desire to join them as one in a way that they hadn't been in a long time overtook him. Moving his hand down to open her legs and wrap them around his waist, he locked eyes with her and kept them there as he slid inside of her body, as slow as he could to allow them both to feel the weight of what they were experiencing. In the back of his mind, he remembered the story she told him of what happened to her and now, like never before, he wanted her to feel and see how much he loved her and that he always would. He wanted to wipe all thoughts and images of that time in her life away and replace them with what love and lovemaking should always be. It doesn't hurt or cause pain, it should fill them both with a love so overpowering that they would never want to be without it again.

"I love you," Aubree whispered.

"And I, you."

"Love me."

"Always," he said knowing words were not enough for him. He wanted to show her and so he started to move. Slow at first until she encouraged him on with her own movements.

They rocked together, moaning and calling each other's names, not rushing, but relishing in the moment, declaring love for an eternity with promises of forever, both of them meaning it.

When Aubree quickened her thrusts beneath him, he held her tight in his arms as she screamed her release louder and with more power than he's ever known from her, he followed her in the same blissfulness state of exhilarating salaciousness, loving her deeper than he had before. He felt one with her, a state of completion, though it was really a new beginning.

As their body's heaved a sigh of relief that they were once again together and ready to fight for their love as one, he didn't make a move to leave the softness of her body. He instead, leaned his head onto her chest and stayed there.

"Never again," Aubree whispered as she kissed his forehead holding him securely in her arms and in her body.

"What?" he asked.

"I promise you that I will never again let our relationship get so bad that I risk losing you."

"Baby, I promise to never again put you in a position to think you don't matter or that I don't desire and love you."

"We'll keep growing together," she added.

"Yes, we'll keep growing together."

Aubree raised his head and this time, she took control of the searing kiss that poured over and through him. He felt her love like never before in that kiss, stirring his body to life once again.

"I want to love you this time," she said against his lips.

Without words, Russell rolled over until she was on top of him and the minute she used her inner muscles to stroke him where they were still intimately connected, everything about him came to life and he knew that their future had to be and he was ready to live in that moment, too – that moment of seizing life as one and never letting go again.

~~

"Oh, my goodness. Is that daylight? Has it always been this bright?" Aubree declared.

"It is and at this time of day, it's brighter than usual and remember the blinds are open."

Aubree yawned and stretched feeling a pleasant soreness between her legs and at the juncture of her thighs that she hadn't experienced in a long time.

"Ooohhh," she muttered, snuggling back into Russell's embrace. She missed mornings like this.

"What's wrong?" he asked.

Aubree looked up into his handsome face where he was already sporting some fresh stubble on his chin, something she was made well aware of as his chin scraped deliciously against her inner thigh sometime throughout the night – more than once. The pleasure of the night and the morning signs had her wiggling her hips to draw even more pleasure from the sensations of their full night of passion. When she thought about the pain in her thighs, she remembered taking control of their loving and using muscles she forgot she had to use to stay on top of him as she took a wild right to ecstasy.

"Nothing's wrong. My body is just reminding me of how wild our desire for each other can get. I can't remember the last time we went pretty much all night and into the morning."

"I couldn't get enough of being inside of you and the fact that we've slept past noon is a sure sign that this was a night to remember," he kidded.

"Noon? It's past noon?"

Sitting up sharply, Aubree reached around for her phone and then remembered she wasn't in their bedroom and that's where her phone was. Not caring, she slid back under the blanket and laid her head on his chest, kissing as much exposed skin as she could find with her lips.

"It's around two and if you're worried about work, I called Jessica earlier when I got up and realized you were still sound asleep. She said she would let your team know that you were taking a day but would be available via phone if they needed anything. Jessica swore she would block all calls to you for today and tomorrow. She also told me to tell you that she's happy for you. What's that about? What's she happy about?"

"I called her last night before I came down here to talk to you."

"Oh?"

Aubree exhaled. It was usually at this point in a conversation with him that she would distract him with sex or change the subject to anything other than a topic that would have her talking about her feelings and what her true thoughts were. She knew that's what had kept them from being together mind, body and spirit as they were the night before and she didn't want to go back to hiding from him. She rolled over on top of his body and rested her chin on his chest, gazing right into his eyes. The hazel pools drew her in. She felt brand new, noticing for the first time just how mesmerizing his gaze was and how his eyes seemed to change colors as she looked at them.

"I told her that I was done trying to seduce you into submission in order to forget about the troubles we were having. I wanted to really talk to you and be open and honest, something that was rare for me. I told her if I called her back, it was because I either chickened out or you rejected me."

"Baby, I would never reject you if I felt that you were finally coming to me without holding anything back. You did that last night and I thank you for doing that. I think it's put us on a new path that may not be perfect, but you can now see that you can be less than perfect with me."

"Yes, and I'm going to continuing working on that part of me. My life has been a rocky road from having parents who didn't want me, leaving me on some church steps like I was trash. If it hadn't been for my adoptive parents, my real parents who took me in at the age of ten after going from one foster home after another, I'm not sure I would know what love was. Then to experience men who never valued me and I allowed myself to be treated as less than what I was worth. I allowed that to carry over into my relationship with you and it was ruining us. For a full day, I sat in that room deciding what I wanted most out of life. Something great was at play in my life, giving me this time with you when we have to tune the world out. Can we stay like this all day? I know we have to eat, but I don't want to move from your arms. I miss being cocooned the way you held me through the night."

"Let's do no television, a little music if you'd like and nothing else but us focusing all of our attention on us. I don't know if we would have done this if it hadn't been for the pandemic locking us all in. I can't say it's a good thing because this virus is nasty, but days, weeks or even months of around the clock being together will allow us to continue seizing every moment possible to remember why we fell in love in the first place."

"I like the sound of that."

"Are you hungry?" Russell asked.

"For food?" she asked mischievously with a wicked smile that told what she had in mind, sore thighs and all.

"I thought you were sore? I know that look."

"I am, a little."

"I'll tell you what. I'm going to draw you a bath with some of your favorite oils so you can soak. We can eat breakfast when you're done and then I can give you a full body massage, focusing on all the places that are a little or maybe even a lot tender and then, I want to act out your dream of us in the kitchen. It sounded hot and sexy, you sounded even hotter and sexier and I'm ready for some role playing. You down?"

"Hell yes! I want all of that."

"Let's get this fun day started!"

Aubree rolled over as Russell moved to get out of bed. She snuggled up to his pillow, inhaling deeply, already missing his presence and his smell and loving the new place they were headed toward in their love. No longer would she play with their love. She was ready to focus on them while leaving everything about the past where it belongs; way back there in her past. Russell wasn't any of her ex's, he was a man who wanted her to know that all he wanted to do was love her. She was ready to fight through her demons and embrace their love.

Seize the Moment
10

"I want to thank everyone for tuning into the show. Did we or did we not have some great guests for you tonight. Wait until you see who I have for you tomorrow. I would tell you, but it's a big surprise. I mean, this is major. I have two guests that never, ever do interviews for anyone, but they're coming on for the Russell Hall show which means I need you to tune in to see who it is. I'm going to give hints for the first ten minutes of the show and the first person to comment on our live with the correct name of the guest will win a special gift from that guest. Are you ready? Yeah, I know you are. Look, y'all know how we do here. We end every show by showcasing an indie music artist and I have a hot one for you tonight. Here, live on the virtual Russell Hall show is new artist, Camille-E, with her dive into highlighting neo-soul music with her up and coming hit, *Days With You*. Check her out and make sure you hit her up on social media to let her know how much you love her new single. This is Russell Hall signing off and giving up the last few minutes of my show to some new stuff. Come back and hang with me tomorrow!

Peace."

And with that, Russell was off the air and he was bone tired. Recently, show executives decided to his show to an actual live broadcast and move away from the pre-recorded show they were doing earlier in the day. Each night during the week, he was up late doing his show and signed off at twelve-forty-five in the morning. He spent his days working on the production of the show and then his evenings doing the show.

As soon as his phone rang and he waved off his team who were finally leaving and heading home for the night, he reached for it, knowing who it was; Brent.

"What's up, bro? Feedback on tonight's show?" he asked.

Brent had gotten into the habit of calling him after every show and given advice on what went wrong and reminding him to stick with things that went right.

"Tonight's show was fire! We got great comments on the live and the sports segment with the tribute to Kobe Bryant with is birthday coming up in August was great. The best idea you had was to set up a basketball college scholarship program in his name. I know he was one of our greatest competitors while also being your hero. You donated the first ten million and the donations have been pouring in all night. We struggled to keep up with the numbers. You should see all of the celebrities donating and your old teammates are really coming through. This is what it's all about. I know you didn't want your show to just be another show. You wanted a platform that would actually touch people's lives and help them come-up. You're doing that, bro. Congratulations! When you win with this show, we all win."

"That's all good news; all good stuff. We've only been on

for a few short months and we are already making a major impact. Tomorrow night during the show, I want share some of the messages we're getting from kids who will be benefiting from the recreation centers that are being upgraded with new equipment and programs so that they will have a place to hang out when it's safe to do so."

Russell wasn't one to pat himself on the back, but this effort was something he was extremely proud about. He was happy to be in a position to bless people around the country while also bringing them the best in entertainment.

"How's Aubree doing? Things still going well? You know I was happy when you told me that you decided to work things out. I knew you would. I couldn't see you walking away from her after all this time. I know how much you love her and despite those troubles, I had a feeling you were going to stick it out because she is worth you; you both are and deserve every bit of happiness."

Russell beamed thinking about Aubree and how good things were growing between them after a rocky road a few months back. They were on a brighter road, brighter than ever before.

"We're still good, man. We talk a lot now and it wasn't until we started really talking and having deep conversations that we realized talking is what was missing from our relationship. We were going through the motions of life together, definitely in love, but I feel like we're now connected on a whole new level. I know I was planning to move out at one time, but I never really wanted to. I didn't want to just go back to what we had knowing that something needed to change. We found out through being in here together more hours in the day than ever before that we weren't putting in the work. We thought we were, but now, we are intentional about that."

"Hey, I told my wife that you and Aubree were working things out and she started dancing around the room and shouting prayer works. She's been praying for you both. You know how much she loves Aubree and you, but still, she loves Aubree more," he kidded.

"Whatever. You know how Aubree and I feel about the two of you."

"Yeah, I do. We've been through a lot together and when I left my job at the tech company to come be a part of your team for the show, I never had a doubt it would be successful. We've been rolling like brothers since college and you know we go from infinity to beyond together. Do you think you and Aubree will work towards getting married now that you're in a better place?"

Russell slouched back in his chair still on the set of the show built in the grand entryway of his house and knew why he and Brent were such good friends. They had minds that were always on the same page.

"I'm already on that. I'm planning something that will involve our families and of course you and Shana. We can't do things the traditional way because of the pandemic, but we can still come together for a moment that I'm planning soon. I'll keep you posted, but yeah, I'm already all over that," he whispered.

"Dude, why the hell are you whispering? Isn't Aubree sleep at this hour?" Brent asked.

"No. I hear her moving around. She tries to stay up to watch the show from our room. I hear water running, so she must be preparing a bath. She's been crazy busy with work and when that happens, she loves a nice, long bath. Speaking of that, I want to join my woman and see if I can do anything to soothe the craziness of her work day. I think she thought, like a lot of people, that working from home would be easier than in the office. I think she works harder here at home. I'm going to go help her relax. We have an early morning meeting with the team to go over tomorrow night's show. I'll holler in the morning."

After his call with Brent, Russell walked throughout the house, locking up and lowering the blinds. He went into the kitchen and grabbed a bottle of champagne he'd put on ice earlier, hoping Aubree would wait up for him as she tries to do most nights not that he was actually doing the show live at night. It was late for considering she had early morning hours and he appreciated how she did everything in her power to support him, even on her most tired of days like today. He was hoping to aid in her relaxation.

Turning off all the lights and securing the alarm, he headed up the stairs and peeped in on Aubree. He found her in a tub of bubbles up to her neck with soft jazz playing. Her hair was pinned up high and her eyes were closed. He knew she wasn't asleep because he could hear her humming to the music.

He didn't disturb her; at least not yet. First, he needed to get in a position to join her, which meant out of his clothes and in the tub with her while carrying glasses of champagne.

"For you, my queen," he said entering the bathroom. When she opened her eyes and smiled up at him, his heart swelled to an unbelievable size. He knew how close he was to not having this scene in his life. This very moment meant everything.

"Aww, you take such good care of me. That's why I love you. I see you're ready for something, I don't know if it's what I'm doing," she commented. His eyes traveled down his body to where her eyes had landed; on his jutting, raging strong and ready, hardened flesh.

"Just thinking about you does this to me," he said and moved in her direction when she reached out for him. Now standing next to the tub, he sucked in a breath the minute her hand reached out and stroked him slowly from tip to base, caressing him in the kind of circular motion he enjoyed.

"Are you relaxing?" she moaned.

When her hands cupped him, he was about to lose his mind, his balance and the glasses he held, one in each hand. The second she leaned over and kissed the tip, he had to move back out of her reach.

"Okay, you're not playing fair. Unless you want shattered glass all over our floor, you'll want to slide up and let me in there with you and we can continue this," he spoke with a voice that was cracking with need.

When she slid forward, he climbed in behind her, sinking all the way down and after placing the glasses on the ledge, he pulled her back toward him, turning her face toward his, he kissed her with solid power and determination. He'd been thinking about her lips and kissing her like this for hours. He couldn't wait to get to her and get to this as he slid his hands down the front of her chest, while his lips continued to kiss, caress and lick at hers.

When his hand fell below the water's surface, he searched for and found her legs open and her womanhood calling out to him for attention. He slid one finger down through her womanly folds before adding another which gave him the squirm and mewling sounds from her that he loved. Her arms going and grasping the back of his neck, holding his mouth in place over hers is what he wanted more than his next breath. He just wanted her and from her response to his touch, she wanted and needed him.

"No words," she whispered against his lips.

The steam from the bath had fogged up all the mirrors and even the glass to the shower to the left of the tub. In between his labored breathing, which matched hers, he delved deeper into the recesses of her mouth, mating with her mouth like a starving man. He was starving. He was starving to never have a moment where he didn't feel like he was feeling right now.

Aubree groaned her pleasure into his mouth as her hips moved from side to side with a little pumping action as he slipped first one, and then a second finger inside of her. That caused her to sigh loudly into his mouth, letting the pleasure of his touch and the heat of the moment take her away to a place that, for a while, he wasn't doing a good job of providing for her. He'd never be caught slipping in that area again.

Needing more and needing to give her more, he turned her body so that she was flush against his chest and in a quick motion, he lifted her up, centered her body over his and then took his time lowering her back down over him until her body completed encased his in the most intimate and erotic way possible. They loved all kinds of positions when making love and one of his favorites was in the tub with her sitting on his lap and then they began to move.

They were so in sync and when she reached down to grip

his strong thighs, her nails dug into his skin, just enough to turn him on as he lifted her up then down while he surged with precise strokes up into her pliant body. She felt hot and it wasn't the water. She gripped him tight and he leaned his head forward and groaned his pleasure into the fleshy part of her back. Her ragged breaths stirred him as they mated frantically, wildly, without regard for the amount of water that sloshed over the sides of the tub that sat in the middle of the bathroom floor. He didn't care. All he needed and cared about was Aubree and the moment they were having with no words, only touches, feels and desire of the mind, spirit and of course, body.

Aubree's body jerked above him as she called out his name again and again. Her voice was soothing, her cries of pleasure as her release surged through her pushed his body more into gear and while bracing his back against the white marbled tub, an amazing flash of light and energy blazed through him and they rode to higher heights together. Aubree placed her hands over his which were holding onto her waist and together they were as one with a mind-numbing cascading wave of pure pleasure. He tried to control his grunts, but the orgasm that was completing shattering him was blinding him. He was completely out of control as his hips pushed up and up and up.

His moment of coming down from his release took longer than he ever remembered it doing before. This moment was powerful – their coming together tonight was how he knew they would forever be one.

On instinct, he wrapped her in his arms as her body calmed and he felt her full weight on him. Her head fell back onto his shoulder and he caressed her thighs, kissing the back of her neck and brought words back into the moment.

"I love you so much. I need you to know that I love you more than anything. I would give up everything in this world if it meant I would always have you, baby."

Russell was overcome with emotions that he felt had been dormant for so long because he hadn't taken much time to just focus on them like this and nothing else. He was focused solely on their pleasure.

"All I need is you," she said. "All I need is you."

Russell felt her moving and when she lifted her body from his, breaking the bond of where they were intimately connected, he helped her turn around until she now straddled his lap, facing him with her legs on either side of him.

Aubree's held the sides of his face, looked deep into his eyes before leaning forward, kissing him sensually, allowing her tongue to glide between his lips, ever so slowly. He took one of her hands and placed it against his chest where his heart was racing. "This will forever be yours. My heart will always be yours. It will love you unconditionally and when it beats, it beats as one with yours," he declared before she leaned forward again and suckled at his lips. She teased him, she took control, this moment was all her.

"I love you, my sweet. Now, forever, for always."

Russell was already ready to take them on a ride to pleasure. When she moved into place, he didn't care what the hour was, that he had to get up early, that she had to get up early; he wasn't letting anything keep them for this kind of blissful love.

Seize the Moment
11

Aubree stood at the island in the kitchen, cutting carrots, celery and onions to add to the chicken stock, pasta and other vegetables that she'd already added to her homemade chicken noddle soup. The weather may be hot outside, extremely hot considering it was the end of August, but not too hot for soup when Russell made special requests of foods he loved that she loved to cook. As she moved around the kitchen, she danced and hummed and was feeling pretty good about herself and about her relationship with Russell that was on a new path since being indoors for the better part of the year and finally putting effort into working on them.

For the past week, he was actually back to work at the studio. Though the virus was still pretty much a big part of everyone's lives, people were learning to cope. With his show back to recording in the studio, though without an audience, he was able to take advantage of the brand-new set along with having his live band on stage with him.

Life for them was good. They spent a countless number of days and nights talking and most of all, reconnecting on a new level. They found a routine of working out together, cooking together and a week ago, after she slept for hours after making love with so much voracity, that she had fallen asleep for hours. When she woke, he had set their dining room up with candles and red rose petals all over the room. There was wine chilling in a bucket of ice, soft music was playing and what excited her the most, was seeing him move around their kitchen like a chef in nothing but a "Kiss the Cook" apron around his waist. He was completely naked underneath. When he attempted to follow the instructions on the apron by lowering herself down his body, he playfully pushed her away telling her she would get her chance to do that after they ate.

While she slept, he'd made them a dinner of braised lamb chops, her favorite, asparagus, another favorite, steamed crab legs and Spanish rice that he made from scratch, not out of a packet. She was thankful that his mother made certain all of her children could cook before they went off to college. They fed each other, talked, danced, kissed and before a desert of banana cheesecake, he made her his desert right on the other end of their dining room table. Now that she knew that it was sturdy enough to hold them both with all the rocking and thrusting they did, she couldn't wait for the next dinner at the dining room table.

Things were really good between them. At her request, he'd found them a couples counselor and for her, someone she could talk to one-on-one to help her deal with her self-esteem issues. The counseling was helping them both and was teaching her how to live and not look back unless it's to give her past the middle finger. They were learning to put each other first, something the pandemic helped them do.

Though he was back in the studio working a few days a week, she was still working from home and loving it. She found more time to spoil Russell to let him know how much she appreciated him and though she had no more plans of micromanaging his in and out of the house, she learned to trust that he really did love her while he took more time staying connected with her when his days were running late, like today.

When he'd called her earlier, he asked if she was in the mood to make him some of her favorite soup. She felt like a kid on Christmas being able to grant his wish. She went out to the store and grabbed everything she would need and came back and began the slow process of making the perfect soup for him. She decided to make a full meal, loving the cookbook that Chrissy Teigen put out with one of Russell's favorite dishes, the famous fried chicken with spicy honey butter. Adding in her very own variety of seasonings that she made herself, she was preparing the perfect meal and was thinking about starting her own line of seasonings. She was ready to up her game and dive back into life without wallowing in what was, instead choosing to live in what is.

Checking her pots and the cake she quickly whipped up and was now ready to come out the oven, she had just closed the oven when she heard the garage door going up. She thought back to a time when she almost lost the love of her life because the sound of the garage door going up irritated her.

"Hey baby!"

Oh, how she loved when he came home, happy to see her.

Aubree turned her head and winked at Russell as he

entered the kitchen and took a seat on the other side of the island.

"Hey! You finish with your meeting already? I was sure you would be a few more hours at the studio," she declared.

"I cut it short. We didn't have a show to record today, just meetings and to celebrate how we are still number one in the ratings for yet another week, toping hosts who have been on the air for years."

"I guess people can't turn away from my gorgeous, hunk of a man. I hope you're hungry because I've been cooking, as you can see from the apron."

Aubree waited until Russell read the words and impatiently waited for him to follow the instructions to kiss her. When he did, it was laced with so much passion that she considered forgetting about the cooking and get something cooking in the bedroom. The kiss ended all too soon and she pouted playfully.

"Don't worry. I have kisses for every part of your body. I am in for the evening and all I want to do is have a nice dinner with you and find something good to watch on television."

"I look forward to that," she answered.

"How was your day? Busy?" Russell asked, snatching up a carrot and nibbled on it as he looked in all the pots on the stove.

"Not too bad. I couldn't wait to get off though. I'm really working on not letting work consume my day. I want more time for us, like tonight."

Aubree smiled over at him and blew a kiss before turning to drop the carrots in the pot and stir it.

"I thought about it as I was driving home. I can now see

what we were missing when it came to time with each other when we had issues. I really didn't realize what I was risking, but not anymore."

"I'm extremely happy about that part. You know, I was just thinking about work and what I would do when the world opens back up again."

"Business owner perhaps? I hope it's the idea around putting out your own cookbooks and finally letting the world taste your incredible seasonings!"

Aubree turned around shocked that they had been thinking along the same lines.

"Get out of my head!" she shouted and laughed out loud. "That's exactly what I've been thinking about. I'm finally realizing what I love doing outside of work and it's cooking and trying different seasonings on old recipes. You think it's a good idea?" she asked.

"I do and I'm thankful that I have a woman who loves to cook."

"You cook too and you're good at it. We should put out a cookbook together!" she offered.

"I'm ready when you are. You know I love to support your ideas. Whatever you need from me, I'm there. I'll even hook you up with the startup costs. I want you to have your dreams. Now that we're back on the same page with our love, it's time we figured out our business and make sure we don't forget the love part in our drive for success. I'd give it all up to not lose the momentum we've gotten back to. I can't believe I didn't recognize how out of hand my drive was," he explained.

"We were both guilty of that and I took it out on you as if you're responsible for my happiness. I am responsible for my happiness and we are responsible for making sure we never stop dating. We were settled in, especially after moving into this house and then the show happened for you and I just found out I made senior partner and they agreed that I wouldn't have to increase my hours, which is great. We were both career hungry, but now, I'm happy that we're back on track, the end of the summer is here and we can get out of the house more than we could months ago. We are in a good place, back in our big bedroom, in our gigantic bed and christening every part of this house again," she laughed. "We are where we should have always been."

"I admit I slipped, but not anymore. You know, my mother practically cursed me out back when this first began. I didn't tell you about that."

Aubree stopped cutting celery and stared at Russell with her mouth hung open. She couldn't imagine his mother, with her sweet nature, even raising her voice.

"She did what? Why?" she asked.

Russell popped another carrot into his mouth that was left sitting on the cutting board before he dove into the story.

"Back in March, I stayed a few days and nights at their house."

"Oh, those nights when I thought you were with another woman and accused you of that? Whew, jealousy is a dangerous thing!" she smiled.

"Ah, you remember that part. I would never share all of this with anyone, but you. You were mad at me, but I still considered us together. Anyway, I finally told her what happened and that I was looking for a condo to move into and she let me have it. Even my dad was shocked!" he exclaimed as he popped a piece of celery into his mouth.

He smiled when Aubree reached into the refrigerator and grabbed a bottle of water to hand to him. She knew him too well and knew that he was about to ask her to hand him one. He opened it immediately and took a long swig.

"Yeah, that wasn't one of my finest moments," she joked. "So, what happened with your mom?"

"She told me to get it together and don't just walk away. She reminded me of all the ups and downs her and my dad went through and how though we were not married, that wasn't an easy out for not working on the relationship. She even went back to my days of playing ball when I was a serial dater and how she couldn't keep up with who I would be seen with next in the media. I told her that I wasn't interested in being serious about a woman when my focus was on my career. I hadn't planned on playing ball for fifteen years, more like ten, so I wanted to get it done and leave my personal life to be built up after playing ball. A few times, I brought a girl home and my mom was just horrible to her – noticing a gold digger when she saw one, according to her," he said.

"What about me? She wasn't mean to me."

"Aubree, my mom loved you and she still does. When I invited you home for Thanksgiving five years ago, you were the first woman I ever took home and at the end of the night, she gave me a thumbs up. You know how blunt my mom can be. She would tell others that it was nice to meet them and she would then wish them a nice life," he sneered and laughed.

"In other words, hello and goodbye! I really love your mother!" Aubree quipped.

"Yeah, yeah. That's because she's always loved you.

Anyway, when I told her that we were breaking up and what happened, she went in. She said she'd waited a long time for me to find the one and she knew it was you and she said that hoping I would realize it too. She called me blind and stupid if I let you walk out of my life all because I couldn't find time to remind you constantly of the love we've always had and how we got to that love. She told me she finally understood me not wanting to get serious about a woman while I played ball, especially with the travel schedule and the appearances from endorsements I'd acquired. What she didn't get was how I was squandering away my relationship with you and not solidifying it the proper way. I told her I had been thinking about that even before you broke up with me. Things just got out of control and I admit, I took it for granted that you would be here, waiting on me to get to the point when I would be ready to give my all to our love just as I was giving to my relationship. I told her I was giving you the house and she told me that the house was the least of what I should have given you in the breakup. She was legitimately pissed off! She was going off on me to the point that my dad walked in, saw her going off and he quietly backed out of the room, leaving me to deal with her wrath. It was crazy, but everything she said was true."

"You know I didn't want your house," she said.

"It's our house and it was ours back then."

"You bought this house with your money. I only pay the household bills and that's because I threatened to leave you if you didn't let me pay something."

"That still bothers me, but I understand. I may have bought this house, but I bought it for us. I saw us living in this house together, forever."

"Me too," Aubree said.

"I was excited about this house. I mean, you did your thing with decorating and turning this house into our home. I felt like you deserved it."

"I don't like talking about what could have happened. We're in a better place now and now one's moving out. We're good," Aubree admitted and leaned over the counter as much as she could. When he saw her intent, Russell leaned over and met her halfway as she kissed him on the lips and moaned when the kiss made her tingle.

"I know we are, but that time back in February and March when we were going through a manic period."

"Yeah, it was strained, but we survived," she said.

"Baby, I'm so glad you came into my life. I don't know where I would be right now. You've made me a better man because that guy was out of control with the serial dating thing."

"You were young and so damn sexy. I can see why women flocked to you, but never again. They don't want to have to deal with me!"

"I know that's right. I'm trying to make sure I stay on your good side. I prefer being in bed with you than in my man cave. This house was my first real big purchase and it was because I knew we had something that I wanted to last. I mean, I made millions and I could have had tons of cars, jewelry, you know, all that stuff the brothers buy to be flashing with admirers foaming at the mouth. I invested a lot and saved a lot which allowed me to retire after all those years while I still have my knees," he said.

"Your knees work just fine," Aubree winked and turned to place the rest of the vegetables she'd cut up in the pot.

"Besides, you're not a big jewelry kind of guy and you have your car and your truck. How many cars can a man actually drive at one time. I know you want to get a boat and I hope you still do. I would love to get out on the water more once all of this is over and not just renting a boat. I love being out on the water and I'm telling you, this pandemic has made me appreciate everything in life a lot more, especially how much I know you love me. You've spoiled me for years and I appreciate you. I really appreciate how you understand you don't have to spend tons of money on things to be accepted by people. I love our life."

Aubree continued stirring in the vegetables.

"Actually, there is one piece of jewelry that I splurged on big time recently, but every dime was well worth the purchase."

"Really? What was that? I love DJ Khaled, but tell me it wasn't one of those medallions that he likes to wear. I know he's your favorite artists right now and you love that GEICO commercial with him in it."

Taking a spoon from on the counter next to the stove, Aubree scooped out some of the broth now that all of the seasoning had been added and blew on the spoon before tasting it. She turned back around to tell Russell just how good the soup tasted and found that he was no longer on the stool on the other side of the counter. Looking to her left, she found him not standing up at his full height, but found him down on one knee holding out a red velvet box, with an off-white satin bow tied around it.

"This," was all Russell said.

Aubree didn't know what to say or what to do. Seeing him down on one knee was unexpected. She could feel her heart palpitating rapidly in her chest as she stared from his eyes, to his bright smile to the box resting in the palm of his hand.

"*Wwwhat* is this?" she finally managed to stutter out.

"Open it and see."

Aubree gasped and as she cupped her mouth in surprise at what was happening, she dropped the wooden spoon to the floor. Before reaching for the box, she already felt tears welling up in her eyes. Russell was on one knee. He was on one knee in their kitchen holding out a box. She tried reaching for it, but her hands were shaking so hard that she pulled it back and held it at her side.

"I...I...Russell, what are you doing?" she asked.

"Baby – open the box," he smiled.

Aubree chuckled as tears finally fell down her cheeks. She let them stay where they rested and focused her attention on the box and on Russell's face.

"Okay," she finally was able to stammer out.

"Now, while you're opening it, I want to say that I love you. I love you so much and I never, ever want you to forget this time in our lives. You and I have literally seized the moment these past few months and took a step back to focus on our love. For the past few years, I took for granted that you would be here loving me and I know that you would continue to do so, but that's not enough for me. I want you to be my wife, the mother of my children, the woman I share the rest of my life with. This pandemic has made me rethink about what I deemed important and at the top of that list is you. You sit right at the top and then everything else trickles down from that. Without you at the top, there is nothing else underneath that could sustain me – not my heart, not my mind and not my love. You do that for me and in seizing this very moment, I want to ask you Aubree Lenay Campbell, will you be my wife and love me just as you always have and allow me to love you for eternity?"

Aubree was really crying now that he's spoken from his heart at the same time as she had finally, with quivering fingers, untied the ribbon and opened the box to find a large princess cut, halo diamond engagement ring set in platinum.

"Oh, my god, this is so beautiful," she cried, barely able to see the ring now that tears really pooled in her eyes."

"Answer him!"

Aubree looked around to see where that came from. She knew the voice. It was her own mother.

"Yeah, answer him!" another voice said.

"Say yes girl!"

This time, she looked at Russell when she knew she recognized his mother's voice and the voice of her best friend, Jessica. When he pointed to his iPad sitting on the counter facing them, she saw that he had connected her mother, father, sister and brother, his best friend Brent and a few of his basketball buddies, Jessica and his own parents as well as his sister and brother. He had connected them all on Zoom. She looked closer and saw cousins and other friends, a few of her co-workers she was close with and even the girl who does her hair.

"When did you do this? We were just talking about food and stuff and I didn't see an iPad. Oh my god! Mommy! Daddy! You're all here!" she shouted.

"Baby? Focus," Russell said and laughed. "I know we talked about my knees, but these thirty-five-year-old knees aren't what they use to be. Soon, I'll need some help to get up if you don't answer," he added.

"Oh, I'm sorry. Yes, baby! Yes, I'll marry you!" Aubree shouted and danced around in place with more excitement than she'd ever felt before. She had no idea he was planning to propose. She was living in the moment and now that the moment included Russell standing and placing an engagement ring on her finger, she couldn't be happier. With the ring in place, she leaped into his arms, wrapped her legs around his waist, kissing him so passionately that she forgot they had spectators.

"Girl – get a room! We don't want to see all that!" Jessica shouted at them.

Aubree ignored her and all the clapping from everyone else. Her mind was on the man who was holding her snug in his arms, kissing her back with as much love and desire that she was laying on him.

"I love you!" she shouted when they broke for air.

"Hold that ring up!" her mother shouted.

Hopping down from his arms, Aubree turned around and showed them the ring in the camera.

"It's beautiful! I can't wait for the wedding. I hate that we're still in this pandemic," Russell's mother exclaimed.

"Stella, I know because you and I need to get together to help plan this," her mother said.

"Sharon, I'll call you. As mother of the bride, you, and the mother of the groom me, we can pull this off even virtually. I hope they're not planning for a long engagement because I want some grandbabies soon," Stella shouted and everyone laughed loudly.

"Me too! Don't leave me out! I want to help plan since I already know I'm going to be that maid of honor," Jessica yelled.

"Ugh, how about me? I'm going to be the bride. I should be included in the planning, don't you all think?" she asked sarcastically.

"I'm so happy for you! When Russell called us all for a Zoom call earlier in the week to tell us he was planning to propose to you, I was crazy over the moon with happiness. It took everything in me to not let the cat out of the bag when I talked to you the other day. I need this pandemic to be over," her mother said.

Aubree leaned back into Russell's arms when he pulled her back to him and held her tight around the waist.

"We're going to make this happen and pandemic or no pandemic, we're not waiting to see when this will be open. We'll work this out," he said.

"We'll let the two of you enjoy this moment. Aubree, call me later. I love you, sweetheart," her father said.

"I love you all, too! Thanks for being a part of this," Aubree said.

With everyone disconnecting, Aubree turned the iPad down and turned back to the man who had definitely seized the moment and solidified their love.

"I don't think everyone had disconnected yet," he said, laughing.

"I don't care. Trust me – they do not want to be an audience to what is about to happen in this kitchen the moment I cut this pot off. We can get back to cooking later. I want to make love to my fiancé right this moment," she declared.

Aubree could hear Russell laughing uncontrollably as she rushed to turn off the stove, took him by the hand and raced for the bedroom steps.

"Baby, what are you doing? Slow down!" he said, rushing to keep up with her fast-moving steps.

"I'm seizing more of this moment and in five minutes, I want you naked. All I want to see is skin and this beautiful diamond on my hand!" she screamed and ran up the steps ahead of him.

Seize the Moment
Epilogue

Russell moved across the make-shift dance floor that he was able to have created in the expanse that was the backyard of the home he shared with Aubree, his wife. She now felt different in his arms than she ever had before. Today had been their wedding day and everything about them felt new.

Aubree was beautiful in her gown made specifically for her by Vera Wang who had it delivered to them in record time. He was not playing when, after making love for the rest of the night after getting engaged, he told Aubree that he wanted to get married in a month. He laughed at her reaction when she thought he was joking, but he wasn't. She thought there was no way they could make a wedding happen in a month in the middle of a pandemic. He showed her just how serious he was. He asked her what her perfect day would look like and he tried his hardest to make it all come true from the decorations to the fact that he was able to charter private jets to fly her parents to Los Angeles along with several other family members who all agreed to be tested for covid and they promised to quarantine until the ceremony. Their closest friends were already living in Los Angeles and with social distancing in place, they were able to have a glamorous wedding. The crowd was smaller than they would have had if it were not for a pandemic, but they had those in attendance who meant the most to them.

Moving with Aubree in his arms to their favorite love song, *For You*, by Kenny Latimore, he knew that he would never see a more perfect day. If not for a pandemic, he would have contracted to have the singer in person, but one day, when the world wasn't so crazy, they would have a big celebration and he would make that contact. The song was nice, but having it sung to his woman would be the icing on the cake.

"Happy?" he leaned down and asked Aubree as they danced.

He watched her look around at their families who were enjoying themselves and when she smiled, he knew he was going to get the answer he was expecting. When she looked up at him, before she could answer, he kissed her lips.

"Happiest day of my life. Thank you, baby. I love you and this day is perfect," she said.

"You're perfect and you look amazing. I know I keep saying it, but you do," he said.

"You look good in a tuxedo. I still can't figure out how you made all this happen," she said.

"Our mothers know how to make things happen. I simply gave them my credit card and told them that money did not matter when it came to this day. What you see is all them and they were able to do it via Zoom and conference calls. They are amazing!" he said.

"You're amazing. You really meant it when you said you

were seizing the moment. I will never forget this moment when I got engaged and married in the midst of a pandemic."

"Baby, anything is possible when the focus is on love. Our love matters. Our forever matters."

"How did you get the band from your show to play and they're doing it in masks?" she asked.

"They know how important this day is to us and when I asked, they couldn't wait to say yes."

"You have them on the other side of the pool and it's so perfect. That makes for such a romantic setting and now that it's nighttime, it looks ever more romantic. And what really topped off the entertainment was how you got DNice and his *Club Quarantine* crew to join us via live on Instagram as he played music to serenade us with our favorite love songs. You are amazing and I love you. No matter what the future holds, when it comes to this pandemic, promise me that we will always seize every opportunity to just love," Aubree asked.

"We will always do that and when we have kids, we'll one day tell them about this pandemic and how our love survived it."

Russell leaned down and pulled Aubree closer when she leaned closer to him.

"Speaking of kids, we're already six weeks along in our plan for babies," she said.

Russell stopped moving, not sure he'd heard her clear.

"What?" he asked louder than he'd planned, but not loud enough to jar anyone else's attention as some ate and others danced.

"You're going to be a daddy in a little over seven months," she said. "I know it wasn't planned," she added.

"Are you serious right now? Don't joke baby. You know

how badly I want kids," he exclaimed.

Russell held it together, but he wanted to run and jump in the pool he was so happy.

"I'm serious and I'm sure. I decided to stop taking the pill so that we could get pregnant thinking it would take a while since I've been on the pill for four years. I didn't think I'd get pregnant that fast. What I have learned is that you are clearly very potent and we'll need to keep birth control around or we'll have twelve kids running around. I don't want to tell anyone yet until we are a little further along. You okay with that?" she asked.

Russell picked her up and spun her around before placing her back on her feet.

"You have made me the happiest man in the world. I know the world is going through something right now that's testing us, but I'm thankful that we can find this happy place that we can carve out just for us. This kind of happiness is what people need. I agree that we shouldn't tell anyone else right now and when you're ready, we'll tell the whole world! I just want this moment between me and you for a little longer. I can't wait to be a daddy. Thank you for being all I need," he said.

"Thank you for being my dream man and not giving up on me or our love."

Being Neighborly
A Short Story

Being Neighborly
1

"This is Levi Ham and I want to thank you, my listeners, for riding with me night after night while I play the best in music for the lover in you. Tonight, I'm going to take it back and we're going to listen to some of the best baby making music of the seventies, eighties and nineties. That's what I keep getting messages about that you want to hear more of. We are on from ten in the evening until two in the morning and you know this isn't just my show – it's *our* show. I play what you like and what you need. Y'all know how I feel about music from that genre. I thought tonight, for the last hour, I'd play your special requests from the likes of Luther Vandross, Prince, Al B. Sure, Teddy P and my favorite of all times, Barry White. That brother was responsible for most of you who listen to my show nightly. Ask your parents! We're going to start with Barry tonight. Reach out for the one you *love*, sit back or lay back and allow your love to get lost in the sweet melodious sounds of *Practice What You Preach*. You know, I get a lot of messages from women asking me if I practice what I preach. Let me just say, you have no idea or maybe a few of you do. I'll let them answer for me. Join me while I'm live on Instagram for the next hour. Let's talk about what practicing what you preach is all about. This is for the grown and sexy, so make sure the kiddies are sound asleep and put your headphones on. This may get hot! Alright, here we go, song number one! I'm Levi Ham with *Beats for the Heart*. Let's go!"

Natalie Banks yawned for the twentieth time. She had just gotten home from her second sixteen-hour shift at Sentara Norfolk General Hospital where she works as the head nurse in the emergency room. Before moving to Norfolk, Virginia six months ago, her usual routine when work went well into the evening when she worked in Charlotte, North Carolina, was to get off, go straight home, get a hot, hot shower and get right in bed, drowning her draining workday in at least ten hours of sleep. That was the case until one night, a few months back, she decided to forgo her usual *SiriusXM* Satellite Radio comedy station, which helped her stay awake on her middle of the night drive home, and instead, she checked out a grown and sexy late hour show hosted by Levi Hamilton, who went by Levi Ham on the radio.

The minute she moved back to Norfolk, her hometown, after her messy divorce from Brant Campbell, her sister, Vanessa had done nothing but rant and rave about this night time show that she claims was making babies all over the country. Vanessa had no proof other than the chatter when Levi would go live on Instagram and men and women would comment that thanks to his slow grinding music, they made baby after baby after even more babies.

Natalie loved her sister but she also blamed Vanessa for her what was a lack of sleep four nights a week when Levi's show aired. It wasn't the music that drew her in, but it was Levi's voice. Tonight, was no different.

The minute she got home, she raced around to prepare for the last hour of his show, something he'd been talking about all week. His show was the best on-air and the chatter on all social media platforms was about, not just the music he played, but the slow, deep, sexy drawl of his voice that mesmerized, hypnotized and held you captive until he signed off. You wanted the music, but more than that, you couldn't wait until the song went off and that voice hit you deep, below the belt, which to her, was as sexy as sexy could get.

Most men had to work hard at deepening their voice to the natural base of Levi's voice. Just listening to him was arousing to the point of erotic release with no touch.

Her mood tonight was definitely on the vibe of erotic. Perhaps it was just his voice or it could be the combination of his voice along with the image of him as he jogged past her townhouse at five in the morning. Even in the winter, like they were in the midst of now, he wore tight gym shorts under basketball shorts and she would watch his muscles flex as his legs pushed in what appeared to her to be him gliding by her house. She watched him as her mind slowed his movements for her until she imagined him running in slow motion. That way, she could get more of a view of him than the flash she really got as he ran by her house fast.

When she watched him, she did so in the dark recesses of her house. She would sneak a peek out of her bedroom window, making sure to hide behind the curtains while getting a look at him through the slits of her blinds. She felt like a stalker, but she also knew that it was all worth it. Disappointment would then settle in because by the time he came back, if she was going in early, she would miss that view. The man was a walking and running Adonis. He often ran with a hoodie on, the one neighborhood where a black man could run with a hoodie and not run into danger. Everyone knew Levi and married or single, the women looked forward to his daily sprints down their street.

It wasn't until a month after she moved into her townhouse that she found out she lived a stone's throw away from Levi Hamilton, the once Olympic track star, now athletic gym owner and nationally known radio personality. She'd done her homework the minute she found out how close to her he actually resided. Her mistake was telling her sister Vanessa, who now, had no problem coming by for unexpected visits in hopes that she would run into Levi, not that she was interested because she'd recently moved in with her boyfriend, Kevin, the love of her life, but no one could resist letting their eyes take in all of Levi.

For one, his voice matched his look. He was sexy, debonair, confident and in every picture she saw of him, he hit the world with an electric smile with perfect teeth and ever-so perfect lips. He was dark chocolate, her favorite and he reminded her of Lance Gross, one of the sexiest actors on the scene. The only difference in the two men was that Levi sported a bald head and she yearned to smooth her hands all across it. Everything about him said perfection, considering the nightmare of a marriage she had come out of. It was great to be able to focus on a man who delighted her with his mere existence.

Happy that she made it home in time to get comfortable

for his show, she grabbed a favorite bottle of wine and her, *"enjoy every moment"* wine glass and after setting the alarm on the house, she rushed upstairs to get ready. Tonight's location for listening to the last hour of his show would be from her bathtub. She had new bubble bath just for the occasion and went right into her bathroom and turned on her iPad to get to her music app. Instantly, the sound of Levi's voice flooded throughout her bedroom and bathroom by way of the strategically placed speakers in both rooms. Some would call this obsessive and she had no problem with that. If they lived as close to the voice over the radio as she did, they would react the same way.

As Barry White's voice serenaded her, she couldn't help but recognize how perfectly Levi's voice mirrored the famous singer, especially when he says, *baby.* Him saying that one words gets her blood flowing, driving her crazy with need and a passionate desire like nothing she'd ever experienced just from a man's voice before.

There were a few times when she would be outside unloading her car or checking her mail and he would drive down the block, roll down the window and wave at her. Over the months, they'd gotten a little more friendly and he would actually stop for a few seconds to say hello and he'd even introduced her to his kids, a boy and a girl, Lennox and Jordyn.

Through their quick chats, she was learning more and more about him, but the times of running into him were few and far in between. Secretly, she was so into him, that the idea of him wreaked havoc on her dreams. With him in them, they were vivid, almost life-like and in the morning, she noticed the evidence of her salacious dreams about him.

They were filled with every sexy thing she heard in the music he played or the air, into her bedroom, into her mind and then all over her body.

Excited seared through her knowing she'd have at least one more hour of that voice and then she would take her party of one to bed and let her imagination bring her a night of satisfaction.

She headed toward the bathroom and quickly removed her clothes as Levi introduced the next song, something by Teddy Pendergrass. She was in heaven. These were artists back before her time, but their music and the impact of it will last forever from one generation to the next. The minute she heard Teddy sing, *"Turn Off the Lights",* she turned the lights off in her bathroom and used the remote to turn on the flameless candles that were place around the tub and across the counter, giving her bathroom a sexy glow. Without any embarrassment, she reached into the secret place in her linen closet and pulled out a sexy toy that would have to substitute for having an actual man in the tub with her, that man, in her mind, being Levi. Was she crazy? Was she overboard with her desire for him? She didn't care. This was Levi Hamilton and if she couldn't have the man in person, her imagination would have to do.

Being Neighborly
2

"Big brother, I wasn't expecting you to be up this early after last night's show. I mean, whew! I've been getting texts from friends all morning who listened to your sexier than ever radio show and let me just say, there was a lot of sexy happening last night because of you."

Levi looked at his sister, Dena, as he stumbled down the stairs after only a few hours of sleep. He'd gotten in so late from the studio that he hadn't even undressed until his morning shower. Usually, he would try and catch a few extra hours of sleep especially leading into his three days off, but his plans changed and he needed to be up early.

"I'm glad everyone liked the show. Did you listen in? I think I saw a few comments from you on the Instagram chat, but the comments were flying by so fast, I couldn't read them all."

"I caught a little bit of the show and I after I started reading the comments, I had to fan myself and remove myself. The women are all over you and seeing those comments about my brother, I felt like I needed to focus my attention elsewhere. You get that all the time?" Dena asked.

Levi smiled to himself as he reached for his favorite coffee mug and placed it under the Keurig spout. He was in dire need of a lift. Last night's broadcast brought on so many celebrities and at one point, he saw his live numbers reach to well over ten thousand, which was crazy and from what his producers told him, that was the low end to the number of people on the live. They had to keep starting it over since they were overwhelming the system. He loves nights like that and his team at work suggested he add a live chat to every broadcast. He agreed as long as they hired him additional help to handle it and they agreed.

"I get it on-air, off-air, even in the supermarket."

"You may need to hire security. I saw what some of the women, and a few men, said they'd like to do to you and you just may get tackled and have your clothes ripped off in public, I'm thinking even in broad daylight. I can't have my baby brother in that kind of situation. I'm sure there is enough clothes being ripped off around this place on the regular."

"First of all, we're twins and you're only two minutes older than me, so stop calling me baby brother. I'm a grown ass man!" he joked.

"Whatever, grown ass man. Why are you up so early? You remembered I was coming over today to use your indoor gym?" she asked.

"Actually, I forgot about that. Nah, I'm up early because I have to pick the kids back up."

"Why? I thought they were staying with Serena and her new husband while they're in town. Isn't she here for two weeks or something like that before they head back out of the country? I don't know how these military folks do this with all this traveling and bouncing around the world and she's a few months pregnant? What gives this time? The last time she was here, something like this happened."

"She called last night just as I got to the studio and said they got a call about a death or something and they needed to go someplace to plan a funeral or attend a funeral or, whatever. I don't even know. She asked if she could bring the kids back a little earlier than planned. I asked if she was coming back before she leaves the country so that she could get a little more time with them and she said she would try," he explained.

Levi heard Dean suck her teeth in disbelief and her response matched his.

He'd met his ex-wife Serena back in the days when he was an Olympic track star. She was part of the military band that played at one of the events and they'd hit it off right away after meeting at a celebratory dinner for his team. He knew she was in the military and he supported that. They maintained a long-distance relationship and saw each other when time permitted. After dating for about a year, he proposed and they got married. He soon learned that military life was not for him. They continued to live separate lives. He thought she would slow down a bit after they had Lennox, but when the military calls, they do so whether there are kids to factor in or not. She then became pregnant with their daughter Jordyn shortly thereafter and when the baby was only a few months old, Serena was gone again and by the time she returned, Jordyn was already a year old. He was willing to stick it out, but being apart for long periods of time, caused them both to stray and sleep with other people.

When the marriage ended, they remained friends, he retained custody of the kids and every now and then, when she was stateside, Serena made time to visit with the kids where he lived in Norfolk. He was expecting her to spend more time bonding with them on this trip for more than the three days they were with her, but she called and he was up, prepared to go pick them back up.

"And she's having another baby with her new husband? Maybe it will work out this time since they are both in the military."

"I don't know, she's sneaky though," he proclaimed.

"Sneaky? How?"

"When I dropped the kids off, her husband wasn't at the hotel. She said he left to run some errands. She proceeded to tell me how things were a little rocky with them and then she let it sort of slip that she missed the kind of intimacy she had with me and that her husband was lacking. She made some comment like if she wasn't pregnant, she wondered if we would have been able to hookup every now and then when she came to town."

"What! Is her husband sure that baby is his?"

"Dena!" Levi shouted and waved his finger at her.

"I know, I'm sorry. I'm just saying that she has some nerve doing that. What did you say?" she asked sly-like.

Levi saw her eyes flutter like she was trying to be serious and funny at the same time.

"Don't even go there. Serena is Jordyn and Lennox's mother and that's it. She's not a very good one, but she tries and I still want them to have as much of a relationship with her as they can get. I did have plans for the two weeks they were going to be with her. She was supposed to take them to school and everything which is why they stayed at a hotel nearby. She wanted the whole experience and wanted to spend some time with them at school, but that's out of the window."

"What did you have planned? I know you're off for a few days from the radio and from running the athletic center you opened up. You said you finally have a full team in place and that you were looking to open a second location."

"Yeah, I was going to do something around here. I want to redo both of their bedrooms, so I was planning on painting and shopping for new furniture. I was planning on have a few of the guys over for some poker, pool and the like. Just some much needed downtime."

"I didn't hear anything about some downtime with a woman. Who are you dating now? I swear, I can't keep up. I know with that show, you're getting invitations to practice what you preach on them."

"Yeah, I told you I get that all the time, but I'm picky about women. Right now, it's all fun, no commitment and just scratching each other's itches. Why are we talking about this?" he asked.

"I'm just asking because I know for your playdates, you send the kids to my place and you haven't done that in a minute. Hey, why don't I take the kids for a few days? What do you think about that? I haven't spent a lot of quality time with them lately and I know you could use a bit of a break considering you have all these plans."

"You sure? You don't have to. You know I'm always good when it comes to my kids; they are my priority."

"Levi, we all know Jordyn and Lennox are your number one priority, but even you can use a break and I'm off for a few days and you should take advantage of it. My spring and summer are always my busiest season at the hair salon and as a silent partner in the salon, you know what business is like as the weather starts getting warm. In the midst of this freezing cold February weather, I can think of plenty of fun things to do with them."

"If you're sure you don't mind, that would be good. By the time they come back, I can have their rooms finished."

"Then it's settled. I'm going to work out and wait around until you get back with the kids. Say, I saw that there is one other black person in your community now. That's a switch from you being the only African American homeowner, from what I can see."

"Yeah, our home owner association meetings are interesting when I walk in and I'm the only black person. Most know who I am and I get a kick out of watching the men fume when their wives and girlfriend let their imaginations run free based on what they hear when they listen to my shows. I encounter a lot of them when I'm out running. Some even plan their runs around mine just to run into me. It's hilarious and I get a kick out of it," he laughed.

"I bet. Do they know that you don't have a shortage of cuties to take up your time and that you don't indulge in other people's property? Have you met the woman I saw down the street? I saw her a few times when I've come over. She's beautiful. I saw her at her mailbox one day and I could have sworn I was looking at Paula Patton the actress who played in one of your favorite movies with Denzel Washington, Déjà vu and one of my favorite movies with Queen Latifah and Common, Just Wright."

Levi had more than seen his new neighbor – he was

continually admiring her from afar. She was more than beautiful, in his opinion. The woman was mouth-watering, breathtaking, exquisite and he saw all of that the first time he saw her and at that time, he'd only gotten a glimpse. Since then, he'd been able to have a little back and forth exchange with her and her voice was soothing, smooth and alluring and he loved hearing the sensual, raspy sound. Dena was right that she looked exactly like Paula Patton, they could be twins, but her voice – that magnificent voice reminded him of Sophia Bush, the actress who was one of the reasons why he watched Chicago PD. His new neighbor definitely had his attention.

"Yeah, I saw her and she is absolutely beautiful. Her name is Natalie."

When he looked over a Dena, she hit him with her usual suspicious look as if she was waiting for him to say more, yet more, never came.

"Is that it?"

"What more were you expecting?" he asked. Levi was doing his best to keep his tone on an even scale. Being twins with Dena meant that she could read him better than anyone else and right now, she was waiting to see or hear more, but he wasn't offering any. Right now, he and Natalie were just neighbors. If there was the possibility of more and he certainly hoped so, he wouldn't tell Dena about it. She would find a way to make friends with Natalie to learn more about her as if he was looking to propose to her.

"Okay, I'm going to let you slide for the moment, but something tells me you're interested in adding that notch to your bedpost. I know your type and she is definitely it."

Levi shook his head in disbelief at her assumption. In his

head, he was objecting to any idea she had that Natalie would be added to the list of women he had a tendency to parade in and out of his life.

"Weren't you going to go workout? I'm about to head out to get the kids and you know how they are when they see you. If you plan to get a full workout in, you better get to it because the second they see you, they are going to want all of your attention. Sometimes, I think they like you more than me," he exclaimed.

"They do!" Dena yelled on her way down the steps to the home gym he had built two years ago that mirrored equipment in any professional gym. Staying fit was an obsession of his.

Sipping on his coffee and checking through more comments from his show last night, he saw a comment and the photo of the woman looked familiar. Sitting his cup down, he tried to zoom in on the photo and then noted the screen name, NurseNat18. When he clicked on the profile, he had to remind himself to breathe. It was her; his neighbor. He clicked through several pictures, feeling like an undercover stalker, but he wanted to see more of her. Whether in pictures or in person, her beauty was evident. Going back to her comment, he read it and smiled:

'It's the voice for me – Levi Ham has THE voice.'

Her words excited him and he wondered if he was reading more into them than what they are. He wasn't a stranger to the power behind his voice. There had been some award given out for the past few years by some blogger and best radio voice went to him every single year. He was all too familiar with words to describe the sound of his voice and the things women tell him that his voice does to them. He's even received thumbs up and kudos from men who've shared stories of how, not only does the sexy music he plays late night for loves has done wonders for their love lives, but also how some women admit to them that it was also the sound of his voice that got them to completion again and again. He thought that odd that a man would confess that to him, but in his opinion, he believed in whatever it takes to get and keep a woman happy in bed. Perhaps, one day, he could find out what make Natalie happy in bed. He was definitely up for finding out what kind of pleasures she's seeking from a man. He hadn't seen any coming or going from her place, but that didn't mean there wasn't one. He was keeping hope alive that one day soon, he'd find out.

Being Neighborly
3

If absentminded was an image, Natalie Banks knew her picture would be front and center. Standing in the middle of her garage in the middle of the winter locked out of her house was not how she planned to spend her day off. There were so many things about her current situation that all she could do was lean against her car and wait for the moment of brain exhaustion to pass while she figured out what to do next. She looked around at the many boxes she could finally put away on the shelves or finally dump all of the Christmas decorations into plastic bins and get them out of the old moving boxes to give her garage some order. Perhaps, on another day, she would have but not today. Today, she had finally forgot to tell herself to turn the lock on the garage door or lower the door guard to prevent it from closing all the way just in case she absentmindedly entered the garage and didn't have her keys, hence her current situation.

"Who forgets to unlock the door before it closes and

locks behind her? Who? Me!" she shouted to herself.

Her first thought was to call her sister, Vanessa or her parents, but when she reached to the back pocket of her blue denim jeans for the first time all morning, her cell phone wasn't in the pocket. As the weight of the situation hit her, her phone began ringing from somewhere in the house, most likely the kitchen, now that she remembered what she was doing before she entered the kitchen. She had taken her phone out to watch cute puppy videos while she cooked herself a breakfast made for a queen of French toast, eggs over medium and crisp bacon, something she didn't get to do often because of her unpredictable schedule as a registered nurse. She was often either working through her evening shift and too tired to get up early to make breakfast or she was running out for an early shift, unable to have the butter and syrup covered deliciousness she loves so much.

She now had to figure out how to get out of the predicament she found herself in. She could open the door to the garage, but with the after the snow, freezing temperature outside, she wouldn't get far in her favorite large, pink and white fluffy bunny slippers and her national hug a nurse day t-shirt. This was the first time she'd locked herself out since moving into her new townhouse six months ago and on many occasions, she told herself to find a place in her garage to keep a key to the door, just in case. This was one of those moments and she hadn't followed through.

The only option she could think of was to ask a neighbor if she could borrow a phone to either call a friend or to call a locksmith.

Pushing the panel on the wall, the door leading outside glided up and a whoosh of freezing air smacked her in the face, though the afternoon was very sunny. She had to shield her eyes against the bright sun which always glistened on her side of the street this early in the afternoon. Once she stepped outside, it was even colder than her garage had been protecting her from. Locking her arms around herself, she walked down the driveway, looking for any signs of neighbors she could ask for help, but not the one next door. She was evil and her family, especially her rude sons, were annoying and thought that her property was an extension of theirs, walking all on it, especially on the grass she kept manicured at all times. Her neighbors across the street were always kind and pleasant and they each made an effort to always greet each other. She decided to try them and headed in the direction of their house, hoping that their cars being parked out front meant they were home.

As soon as she reached the curb, a familiar, large black SUV pulled up and stopped right in front of her. Even with the windows tinted to the darkest setting, she knew who was on the other side of the glass as it lowered. Plastering a smile on her face against the cold that had already begun to free her facial features in place, she walked closer to the truck and waited the few seconds for the face of Levi Hamilton to grace her with his presence and a fine presence it was. He was her neighbor and though he didn't live on the court with the townhouses, at the end of her court began a group of gorgeous single-family homes. His was visible from her driveway and without realizing it, each time she drove out of her garage and looked in that direction, she checked for his truck which was always parked outside, assuming because of its large size, it wouldn't fit all the way in his garage. He also owned a sleek, black late model, BMW 750, her favorite car and in the evening, especially on the weekends, she would see him cruising down her street in it.

From the moment he first introduced himself, she'd been obsessed with catching a glimpse of him every chance she got, especially when he did his daily run early in the morning. When she had the early shift, she shamelessly stood at her living room window and waited for him to pass by. She wanted to wait for another view whenever he returned, but she missed it because she then had to rush out to work. Levi was so good looking that the idea of any other man being as handsome escaped her. She couldn't think of one. She wasn't the only woman on the block who noticed him; she was, however, the only single woman on the block who noticed him. Everyone else was married but still ogled him just as much or even more than she did. He was definitely a fine chocolate delight who had to be created just so women could ogle him, fantasize about him and for anything else a woman could think of to do with a virile, sexy man like him.

"Hey beautiful!" he said to her and Natalie practically melted to the freezing ground. The voice of the man who'd gotten her to completion in her tub the night before was now right in front of her and if it wasn't so cold out, he may realize the redness of her cheeks was from embarrassment and her imagination going wild and not just from the cold. Why did he have to have a voice so deep that it wafted around her like a bubble of desire. She was feeling all hot and sexy just listening to him speak.

"Hey, Levi."

"What are you doing out here with no coat on and those cute slippers. My daughter has a pair like that," he said.

"Jordyn, right?" she asked, trying to remember his daughter's name.

"Correct. I don't want to hold you up. I know it's freezing out here. Are you good?" he asked.

Natalie looked at him and then back to her garage where she knew she couldn't get inside. She hated to ask, but she was desperate and right now, he was here.

"Actually, not really. I sort of locked myself out of my house. See, I was putting the trash in the can and I forgot to put the door stopper down to keep it from shutting behind me and I usually either take my keys with me or I make sure the lock is disabled and I forgot both. It's been on the back of my mind since I moved in to come up with a plan for when I lock myself out, though I've never done that before now," she rattled on and then stopped when she realized she was saying more than she needed to.

"Perhaps a hidden place in your garage? That's what I do or maybe one of those locks with the key pad instead of a key. I have the keypad because my son has done the same thing when he puts the trash in the bin in the garage. Did you call someone? Are they on the way?" Levi asked.

Natalie found herself unable to pay attention to what he was saying. The way he looked so perfectly comfortable leaning back with one hand on his thigh and the other on the steering, all she could think about was the hand on his thigh. For a second, she let her gaze shift just beyond the hand on his thigh and her eyes widened. Was that all him?

Shaking it off, she looked back to Levi's face and found him grinning at her from ear to ear. Damn, he's sexy!

"Uh, what did you say?"

"I asked if someone was coming to help you."

"Oh, no. I was going across the street to ask the Stewarts if I could use their phone to call my sister or my parents. They all have keys to my house."

"Use my cell. Come sit in the car where it's nice and hot – I mean nice and warm."

"Don't you have to pick up your kids?"

"I do, but I'm heading out early, so I have plenty of time. Come on in."

Before she could reply, Levi had unlocked the car door and reached over and opened the front passenger side door for her. She rushed around, climbed up inside and rubbed her hands together to shake off the coldness.

"It's freezing out there."

"It's a good thing I came by."

She smiled as Levi handed her his cell phone. She called her sister's number while he pulled his truck over to the spot in front of her house and put his truck in park.

"Van, I need your help. I locked myself out of the house and don't ask me how. I need you to bring your key to let me in. What do you mean did I call dad? I'm calling you and besides, you live closer than mom and dad do and I don't want one of his lectures."

As she listened to Vanessa playfully berate her, she glanced to her left and what she saw hand her tingling all over. Instead of Levi's eyes being ahead on maybe even on her face, his eyes were focused on her breasts and he wasn't even trying to hide where his gaze was focused. She lost all train of thought when she saw his tongue slide out and lick across his lips while his eyes were still focused on her chest. She didn't know if he meant to do all of that but it was one of the most erotic moments of her life. Had it been that long since a man ogled her so obviously that the mere idea of it turned her on.

"What? Oh, how long? An hour? Why so long? What are you doing?" she asked.

"She's going to be an hour?" Levi whispered.

"Yes, I'm sorry. I don't mean to hold you up. I'll let you go and just wait in the garage. It's not so cold by the door that leads into the house."

"Nonsense. Tell her an hour is okay. You can ride with me while I pick up the kids and that way, by the time we get back, she'll be here. How's that?"

"Go with you to pick up your kids? Will their mother have any issues with me being in the car?" she asked presumptuously.

"Why would she? She has a man and she's about four or five months pregnant with their first child. I would say it wouldn't matter and if it did, it's not a problem for me. It's not like we're dating or anything and if we were, it would still be okay. I can't leave you standing in a garage in the freezing cold. You can lock your garage. I'm assuming there's not pot cooking or anything?"

"No, just the television in my family room."

"Are you sure I won't be an inconvenience?"

"I'm positive. Tell your sister if she arrives before you get back, to not worry. We won't be long."

"Van, an hour is fine. If I'm not here when you get here, just wait. I can't stand out in the cold."

"Where are you going? To a neighbor's house?" she asked.

"No. I am, um, one of my neighbors was driving by and offered to let me take a ride with him to get out of the cold."

"Neighbor? What neighbor? Wait, is it that sexy one you told me about? Tell me it's him!"

"Van, I'll see you when you get here. I am on his phone and have to give it back."

She kept eyeing Levi, hoping he couldn't hear Vanessa on the other end.

"How hot and sexy is he close up? I bet you want more than a car ride? Is it him? Tell me or I'm going to call this number back and ask."

"You better not! I will kill you and yes, it is."

Without waiting for Vanessa to respond and scream any louder, she ended the call and handed the phone back to Levi.

"Thanks for that. My sister would have continued talking. I'll go lock my garage using the keypad and I'll be right back."

"If you want, I can stop by the hardware store and grab that keypad door lock for you and even install it for you, just in case this happens again and I'm not driving by. I would hate for a woman as sexy as you to be left out in the cold."

"Are you sure? You're doing so much for me now."

"It's not a problem."

Natalie got out and rushed to key in her code to shut and lock the garage door. Not waiting for it to shut, she raced back to the truck and hopped back in.

"I look ridiculous in this get up. I have on fluffy slippers and no coat."

Levi reached behind her seat and pulled a jacket from the back seat and handed it to her.

"Now, you'll be sexy with a boss leather bomber on."

Taking it, she slipped it over her arms and rubbed her

hands up and down the buttery soft brown leather.

"This is nice."

"You look good in it."

As the truck moved, she was now at a loss for words and the silence was going to kill her if they weren't talking. Her thoughts about him were so dirty and nasty from the images of him in his running gear running back and forth up her street that she would stand and watch him as if she was watching a movie – a few times with a bag of chips just like she would do at the movies. The man was too hot to not get a look at every single time.

"So, how old are your kids?"

"Jordyn is six and Lennox is seven."

"And they live with you? I'm sorry, am I asking too many questions about your personal life? I don't mean to."

"It's okay. Yes, they live with me. They spend most weekends with my parents and when their mother is in town, they spend a lot of time with her, but I have custody and have had it since they were born. With their military careers, they do a lot of moving around and I wanted and offered more stability for my kids. You know, you should get one of those keypads for your inner garage door, the kind you can key in to get inside. That way, if you lock yourself out by mistake, you won't need a key."

"I didn't think about that. That's a good idea and clearly, I'm prone to making that mistake."

"It's also good if you have someone coming over and you don't feel like walking to let them in. If they have the outside keypad code and the code to the door, they could simply and easily come in. I have it and I love it."

"I'm sold. I'm going to get that later today once my sister

lets me back into my own house," she joked.

"If you need my help, I can stop you by the store and pick it up and install it. You can program it yourself. It's fairly easy."

"Oh, you don't have to do that. I can get my father to do it."

"What about your boyfriend? He wouldn't help with that?" Levi asked.

Natalie knew when a man was fishing and Levi was definitely doing that.

"I don't have one at the moment. I'm pretty much focused on me right now, no time for relationships," she noted.

"Sounds a lot like me. With the kids and work, I find it hard to have a serious relationship."

Natalie kept her eyes on the road. The moment he mentioned relationships, she couldn't help imagining how he would be with a woman. From the side of her eye, she looked at his hands, nice strong, powerful. She checked out how he sat when he drove and the word that came to mind was confident and secure. She got that vibe every time she saw him. She looked down at his legs and prayed he couldn't see her. She shifted a little when an uncomfortable feeling hit her smack in between her legs. There was something hot and sexy about a man with strong, toned legs. Even in jeans, she could see his legs bulging, not with fat, but with muscle. When the word muscle hit her brain, she went there. She let her eyes drift to his muscle and she couldn't believe the imprint was real. No way was that thing real, she thought.

"No."

"Did you say something?" Levi asked.

"Oh, um, no. I don't know why I said that."

"So, tell me, how do you like the neighborhood, starting with your grumpy ass neighbor. People talk about how busy she is in everyone's business and how she looks down on everybody."

"Yeah, I discovered early that she's just not a nice person. I steer clear of her. I'm about to have a privacy fence put in outback. When her boys congregate in the common area behind our houses, they someone end up in my yard which I can't stand. They're rude, but I'm usually in my house anyway, so it's all good. In all, it's a nice neighborhood. Everyone else seems nice and you've always been nice. How long have you lived here?" she asked.

She secretly hoped he hadn't been there long so that she was assured she would continue to catch sightings of him. She couldn't wait until the summer to see how much more of him she could get a glimpse of.

"I've been here about five years. You'll get to know a lot of them. A few have parties and invite everyone. I do that a few times throughout the year."

"That sounds like fun. Do you play the same kind of music at your parties that you play on your radio show?"

Natalie started to feel regret over bringing up his show considering the sexually stimulating nature of it, but she couldn't help herself.

"Ah, you listen to my show often?" he asked.

"I try to catch it when I can. It depends on my work schedule at the hospital. Yes, nurse Natalie. That has a ring to it."

"Thank you. I like what I do and I look forward to meeting nice people in the community," she replied.

"It's a good way of being neighborly. Are you neighborly, Natalie?" Levi asked.

She started to answer, but when his eyes traveled down her body and then back up to rest on her breasts, desire like none she'd ever experienced before shot through her, especially while sitting and waiting for the light to change, he locked his eyes on hers and she could swear that as she looked at him, his eyes had turned the deepest shade of black from a much lighter gray. Did she actually see that?

Turning her attention back to anything happening outside the car through the front window, she pointed to the light so that he would know it changed.

"I think I'm neighborly. At least I try to be."

"So, you would offer a brother a cup of sugar if he needed it? You know, all neighborly like?"

He was flirting. Hell, she knew flirting and he was boldly flirting with her. Was he really talking about sugar? She was excited and tempted to even flirt back.

"I would if he needed it," she said.

The car was suddenly hot as they sped through traffic, not on the expressway. Where had the sudden influx of heat come from? Was it the car or was it just her?

"What about if he just wanted it? He may not need sugar, but he may have a strong taste for some sugar every now and then. Still neighborly?"

When she looked his way, the smile she caught was a sly one. Yes, there was some flirting going on and she made the mistake of looking back down toward his lap and the slight bulge she saw before was longer and more pronounced. Not only was he flirting, but he was clearly aroused. Knowing that had her womanhood doing its own version of involuntary kegels. The feeling was amazing. She was so turned on that if he asked her if he could pull over and show her how neighborly he could be right now, she would most certainly let him. That was out of character for her, but there was something about being this close to him and knowing that he was aroused drove her desire for him through the stratosphere. He didn't know that he was making her feel sexier than she's ever felt before. No man, using just words, had her aroused to the point that any minute, she may explode and he wasn't even touching her. That's a serious gift!

"I'm sure I would be. It's just sugar, right and we all have it," she said. She was trying her best to keep up with the conversation in hopes that they weren't really talking about sugar but if he was, she didn't want to embarrass herself.

"Some sugar is way better than another kind of sugar. I happen to like my extremely sweet. Do you have that kind of sugar at your house?"

Natalie was about to answer with something witty, once she thought of it, but then they pulled up to a hotel and he found a parking spot near the entrance.

"We're here," said. "That was quick."

"Do you like getting places fast?" Levi asked her.

Natalie knew that she should not be enjoying this as much as she was, but they had gone from zero to a heat factor not even on a measuring scale and she wanted to keep going. She looked his way and smiled.

"Fast is okay, but it's not the preferred speed, in my book that is."

"Damn, I like you. Hold any more thought. I'll be back in a minute after I step out of this truck to get a cold wind shower."

When he hopped out, she let her eyes follow him all the way to the door. She chuckled to herself when she saw him sneak and adjust himself in his jeans. Yeah, she did that and she was happy about it. Natalie had no clue of what came over her. All she knew was her hot neighbor was flirty and not subtly. He was laying it on heavy and she was here for all of it.

Being Neighborly
4

Levi wished he could have continued his conversation with Natalie, but once he picked up the kids and they were in the back seat, he had to stop what he was doing. At first, he thought he was going a bit far when he started the conversation about sugar. He only did so because he caught her looking between his legs and knew she liked what she saw. He wasn't looking at her but he could see her eyes rise to the occasion just as his penis stretched under her perusal. Clearly, she was interested in more than just a car ride and from the second he saw her moving into the neighborhood, he was just as interested in her as she was in him. The looks she gave him, he got from women every day, but there was something special about it coming from Natalie. Something about her told him that there was a magnetic chemistry between them that now that he knew of her, he wanted her.

After dropping his kids off at home first since his sister was there waiting on them, he picked up his toolbox from his garage and drove down the block to Natalie's house and parked so that he could install the new keypad entry pad in her garage. As soon as he parked, Natalie's front door opened and a young woman came sashaying out to meet them just as they were getting out.

"It's about time you got here!"

"Oh, please, miss, I'm going to be an hour when your apartment is only a few miles away. Levi, this is my sister, Vanessa. Vanessa, this is Levi, one of my neighbors," she explained.

Levi put his hand out for a shake and looked confused when she didn't shake it in return.

"I know exactly who Levi is and I'm hoping I can at least have a hug. I feel like we're family I listen to your radio show so much. Imagine that. My sister lives down the block from the hottest man on the radio. Just wow!" Vanessa shouted.

"Um, it's freezing out here – can you continue ogling him from inside the house, please?"

"He's coming inside? Oh, what a treat! I've always wanted to meet you. I'm thinking about going into the radio personality business," Vanessa admitted as she followed Natalie through the front door.

"No, she isn't," Natalie quickly responded.

"Yes, I am. You don't know what I want to do."

"No, you're not. Every time I talk to you, you have some new career you want to pursue and these ideas change with the weather."

"Well, I could have gone into entertainment, but with my degree in accounting, I'm sticking with that for a while so that daddy doesn't think I wasted his money on my college degree in accounting only to change it up and go back to school."

Levi listened to the exchange between the two sisters and

laughed. They sounded a lot like him and Dena.

"Is this your usual chatter. The two of you are hilarious," he said, following Natalie and admiring everything about her.

"Whose jacket is that?" Vanessa asked.

"Van, this is not your chance to play twenty questions. Levi has graciously offered to change the lock on my garage door that leads into the house so that I won't have a problem getting back into my house because I locked myself out. I'm getting one of those locks with the keypad. I would just have to key in my code and the door will open."

"Great, because I may not be around to let you in again and it's too cold for you to freeze outside."

"If it happens again, I don't have a problem giving you another ride until your sister shows up," he added.

The image of him giving her a real ride crossed his mind. He was about to clear up what he said when the double-entendre, the double meaning, hit both sisters at the same time and they turned to him. He caught Natalie's quick blush before she looked away, but clearly, Vanessa was the bold one. She looked at him, smiled and then winked.

"Well, your ride today was the first ride that my sister has had in a very, very long time."

"Vanessa! Go home!" Natalie shouted and when Levi laughed and smiled, Natalie looked at him and blushed even more.

"Alright, alright, I'm going. Call me later because I'll have a lot of questions. It was nice to meet you Levi. Hey sis, are you going to invite Levi to your game night tomorrow evening? I think that would be a nice gesture to thanking him for helping you today."

Game night? Levi wondered what that was about.

"He may be too busy or something, but if you're free, Levi, I'm having some people over for foods, card and board games. I haven't had anyone over since I moved in and my friends have been bugging me about getting a look at the house. You're more than welcome to attend and even invite a few of your friends if you want to. It's all casual," she said.

"I'd love to join you. I'm off for a few days and my sister will have the kids. Are you sure you're okay with me joining?" he asked.

"She is and not just because I brought it up."

"Vanessa, you're still here? Thanks for coming by and I'll call you later."

"Okay, I get the message. I guess I'll see you tomorrow night then, Levi. It has been wonderful making your acquaintance."

This time, Vanessa put her hand out for a shake and he leaned into her for a hug.

"We're like family, right?" he asked and they all laughed. "I better get to that lock," he said walking around them both and going through the door to the garage.

Second later, Natalie joined him just as he was opening the door to prop it open to get the current lock out.

"Do you need anything?" she asked.

"No, I have all the tools I need."

As soon as the words left his mouth, Levi bent down and focused on the door lock. He hoped she took more from his words just like he has. He loved flirting with her and watching her blush. It was sexy; she was sexy.

"Can I get you something to drink? A bottle of water?" she asked.

"Sure. Water would be great."

When she walked around him into the house, he watched her walk. A woman with as much of a bow to her legs as he had and damn, he was going crazy watching her. Everything about her turned him on and his mind couldn't stop thinking about those legs wrapped around his waist or perhaps around his head. When she returned and handed the bottle to him, he wanted to pour the cold liquid over his head to calm his raging body.

He never slacked when it came to having a woman when he wanted one in his bed and he knew a beautiful woman when he saw and wanted one, but Natalie was in a class all by herself. There was something not just sexy, but also sweet with a hint of vixen.

"Thanks for suggesting this lock. It never dawned on me what a great idea having this kind was. I may get one for the front door also. Makes like so much easier."

"Yeah, I have them on all of my doors. They're great to have. If you want me to pick up another for you, let me know. I'm always at the hardware store. I'm about to redo both of my kids' rooms which means I'll be spending a lot of days at the store getting supplies."

"If it's not too much trouble, I would appreciate that. Sometimes, living alone, it's hard knowing who to trust to hire to do work, even something as simple as replacing a door lock. I had a man come to give me estimate on changing the flooring in three rooms from carpet to hardwood. I think he got the vibe that I live here alone. His estimate, to me, was pretty high. I got two additional estimates and his was two thousand, two hundred dollars more than the other two."

"Men can be shady like that. They will get over if they

can. If you still need that done, I have a guy who is a friend who owns his own business doing flooring and carpet installation. I can put you in touch with him."

"That would be wonderful. You are a regular ol' handyman yourself," she said.

Now that they were alone, he wasn't ready to miss an opportunity to really flirt in order to see how receptive she would be. He stood and turned toward her where she was now leaning against her burgundy Lexus truck.

"I'm all kinds of handy. It really depends on what's needed. Do you have anything else you need done?"

The eyes. Her eyes were piercing right through him and then she looked away. He loved the subtly of shyness in her. He would work with that. Shy women turned out to be the most vivacious.

"I guess it depends on what you're talking about. I don't want to assume," she said.

Assume away, is what he wanted to say, but didn't.

"It's the voice for me," he said instead, hoping to not seem too out of place by making reference to her comment during the live chat during his show the night before.

"What?"

He saw her recollection and the look on her face was priceless.

"Wasn't that you on my live last night? The comment about my voice? I didn't see it until I was going through the comments this morning. I love knowing what my listeners think so that I know how to cater to what they want to hear and how they want the show to go. I saw your picture and recognized you. I'm not sure I've ever seen you comment before or I missed it. So? What about the voice is it exactly?"

he asked.

"You saw that?"

"I did."

"It was my first time commenting," she admitted.

"How long have you been listening?" he asked.

"About six months. Since I moved here. My sister told me about the show. I work late and usually listen to comedy when I'm driving home just to make sure, if I'm a little tired, that I don't fall asleep."

"My show puts you sleep?"

"Not at all. I'm wider awake when I'm driving home listening to your show than I do when I listen to anything else. There is something about your voice and I know you know that already. I am not the first woman to comment on it."

"No, you're not, but I want to know what you think."

"Are you flirting with me?" she asked.

"Were you flirting with me in the car when I was flirting with you then?"

This moment would determine his next move. He saw her shifting from one leg to another and she couldn't quite figure out what to do with her hands. She finally leaned back against her truck and placed her hands behind her to keep them still.

"You're serious, right? Have you ever met a woman who hasn't flirted with you?" she asked.

"Not really, but I'm asking you. Was my flirting with you in vain? Was it too subtle because if so, I can be much more upfront, if that works better?"

"You do not have to flirt, I'm sure. I saw the comments last night and women are bold, frank even about exactly what they like about you."

"Yeah, and you said it was the voice for you. I like that kind of subtle boldness. It was there, but not a pointed as other comments, yet yours stood out. Do I make you nervous? Uncomfortable? That's not my intention, but you look sort of nervous as if any minute, you're going to run in the house," he joked.

"No, no, not at all. I'm a little flustered. Have you seen yourself?" she asked.

Levi couldn't stop the loud roar of laughter that escaped his mouth even if he tried. He was liking her more by the second.

"I have. Have you seen you? Men don't flirt with you often? If not, they must be blind."

"I get my share but none are Levi Hamilton."

"What does that mean? I can't be interested in you because of who I am?" he asked.

One thing he noticed about his dating life was that women often shied away from him thinking that because other women found him appealing that he would not be good relationship material because women threw themselves at him every day all day. He hoped she didn't find him unappealing because he was popular. He didn't see her that way, but that was a man thing. Nothing kept a man from being interested in a woman as sexy as her.

"I didn't mean that."

"I know you didn't. I'm just being neighborly and pulling your leg. Look, why don't I finish this lock and I'm definitely accepting the invitation to your party tomorrow night. Maybe we can talk more then. I think you're beautiful and let me just say that I'd like to talk more about what my voice does to you. I'm intrigued," he said.

"Have you always been this neighborly?" Natalie asked him.

"Not with anyone around here, but I've had my share of being neighborly and I find it fun when the neighbor is friendly and sexy. I don't shy away from a woman I see I'm interested in. I do admit that I'm not in search of a girlfriend, a wife or a mother for my kids, but I'm an adult and so are the women. I always say, why not be bold when the reception you get may be what you're really asking for without actually asking for it."

Natalie cleared her throat and he should be offering her a bottle of water. She was more than flustered at how straight he was being and she was reading him loud and clear.

"Do you enjoy being neighborly?" he asked, curiously.

"I've never been neighborly, but I wouldn't count it out; at least not at this moment."

Her eyes. There they were again. They spoke volumes and if there was a woman who looked at him with a deep desire to see what his meaning of being neighborly was, it was her and he was up for the challenge.

Being Neighborly
5

The party was in full swing and Natalie rushed about making sure the food stations were fully stocked and thanks to Vanessa's boyfriend who was a part-time bartender with his own mobile bar, the drinks were flowing and music played throughout the house. She looked nervously at the door every time someone rang the doorbell. So far, there was no sign of Levi and she hoped he was still coming.

The day before, they flirted briefly, dancing around using the word sex in their conversation but it sat there in the middle between them. There was something so sexy and virile about a man who spoke his mind and let it be known what he wanted and he definitely wanted her. Her sex life, in the past, had been pretty dismal, even with her husband.

She had been in a marriage, albeit, a brief two years, it was a rough two years. Nothing about the marriage satisfied her, especially intimacy. She got married because she thought they had been in a relationship for three years and the next natural thing was marriage. Even though the sex wasn't that great, it got worse after they were married. She was left wanting and would never admit to anyone that she faked orgasms more times than she could count. Why she did that to herself, she didn't know, but that was over and done with and the divorce was bitter on her ex's part. He thought that she didn't do her part in making it work and she knew she never should have married him simply because he asked. What Levi exuded was pure, raw, animal attraction and her mind and body reacted in a way that was foreign to her. She was excited about him coming to the party. She'd taken all day to figure out what to wear and finally decided on white button down top that she tied tight under her breasts. Under that, she added a black tank top and black leggings, an outfit that was made for comfort and all the running around she would be doing. She looked up just as Vanessa was bringing more plates and glasses from the lower level where the party was in full swing with the twelve or so guests.

"Hey sis! This party is everything. I am having a good time. Thanks for inviting me. I know you like to hang with your friends without your annoying little sister around. I came to make sure you are enjoying yourself," Vanessa said moving about picking up empty cups and plates from a table near the sliding glass door.

"I'm glad you're enjoying yourself. I have some new trays of food and desserts. Can you help me put them out?" Natalie asked, trying to distract herself as she waited for Levi to show up.

"Sure, I got you covered. No Levi yet? Did you really invite him or did you take back that invite after I left? You know you want him here and you know you want him. The two of you could barely keep your eyes off of each other yesterday. I thought that any minute, you would drop and get busy right in the middle of the floor. There is fire between you two. Are you going to do anything about it?" Vanessa kidded.

"Stop playing with me and get out of here with that. There was no fire. You were seeing things."

"Sis, don't even go there. I know that look. I never saw it with you and Brant, but I saw it with you and Levi and I could feel the electricity between you two. You are a fool if you don't get a little taste of that. Do you have any idea of the number of women who want to get with him? He's single, gorgeous and has eyes for my big sister. Get you some and don't look back. You need some fire like him in your life after that fake marriage with Brant. I don't know why you married that stale brother. Now that it's over, get you some real, good lovin' and from what I hear, Levi has it going on. Women talk and it's all good. He gets no bad press. Can you imagine a man as sexy as that with women clawing at him and not one of them has a bad word to say? In fact, I read someplace that the brother is really packing!"

"Van, if you don't shut up!" Natalie said with a smile. She couldn't fake being mad if she tried. She'd read some of the comments about Levi and she felt like a spy on his sexual prowess, but Vanessa was right – women who claim to have been with him raved about him, no bad press and most wanted more, but he wasn't into that and made that known before they indulged in anything. That's what she would like in her life right now. A man to just enjoy with no pressure of anything more than just great, headboard knocking, clawing at the sheets, screaming like a banshee kind of sex. Would Levi be interested in something like that with her?

Just as she was thinking about him, the doorbell rang and she looked into the monitor on the kitchen wall and saw him and he had a friend with him; a male friend.

She sighed with relief that he didn't bring a woman. She told him he could bring whomever he wanted and she hoped it wouldn't be a female.

"Is that him?" Vanessa asked, running over trying to get a look in the camera.

"Yes, and take the tray downstairs. I'll get the door."

"I bet you will," Vanessa said to her and then ran for the steps before Natalie could chastise her playfully.

Smoothing her hands down her hair and down herself to check for any clothes out of place, she rushed for the door.

As soon as she opened it, Levi smiled at her like they were long lost friends who hadn't seen each other in years.

"You made it," she said, moving to let them in. The minute he walked by, she caught a whiff of his column and the manly scent tickled her nose. She immediately thought of other ways she'd love to be tickled by him. He was hot as fire in a black leather bomber jacket, blue denim jeans, black, thick leather boots and on his head, he wore an all-black, Worth & Worth men's Fellini hat. Goodness the man was a walking fashion magazine.

"I did. I wouldn't miss another chance to see you, beautiful," he said.

When he leaned over and kissed her on the cheek, she shivered from the contact. Maybe Vanessa was right about the fire between them because all of a sudden, the temperature in the room rose several degrees or it was probably just her body's heat.

"Were you waiting for me?" he whispered so close to her ear that she knew his guest or anyone else heard him.

Looking around, she checked to see if anyone was

watching as people milled about. Noting no one paying attention, she leaned up as he leaned down to hear what she had to say.

"Yes."

She gave him one word and a smile and then turned to his guest.

"Natalie, this is my best friend, Byron. I hope it's okay that I brought him. He wasn't doing anything tonight and I thought he'd have a great time. We also brought two bottles of wine. I hope that's okay. I know you said not to bring anything, but I can't show up at someone's house and not bring something. I had to be neighborly," he said.

Natalie thought back to their conversation in the car when he asked her if she was neighborly. She sure wanted to be; with him.

"It's nice to meet you, Byron. Thank you for the gesture. Everyone will love the wine. There are a lot of drinkers here tonight. Come on in, hand me your jackets and the party is on this level and the one downstairs. There are three rooms downstairs. In one, they are playing card games like spades and something else. The other they are playing board games and in the main room when you first get down there, it's a melting pot of stuff. I think they are about to play this board game I bought called, *'Slide in Your DMs'* or something like that."

"Oh, that sounds like fun – like my kind of game. You don't want to play?" Levi asked her, joining her as she walked toward the kitchen.

"Yes. I was just picking up more food to take downstairs. Get something to eat. There is food up here and downstairs. My sister's boyfriend has a mobile bar set up downstairs.

Byron, do you mind taking the wine you and Levi brought and handing it to the bartender downstairs?" she asked.

"Gotcha," Byron said, taking the bottles and heading toward the steps.

"Just you and me now. I'm looking forward to unwinding tonight. I love game parties. Maybe later, you can give me a tour of the rest of your house," he said.

"I would love to."

"Great. Let me help you with these trays. You look amazing tonight," he said.

Natalie didn't want to play circles around her interest in him. Vanessa was right about one thing. The man was sexy and why shouldn't she have a taste if he was interested. She went for it.

"I would tell you what I think about how you look, but I'll save that for later," as she winked and walked ahead of him, noting how his eyes traveled her body and landed on her behind. His eyes burned through her, raising the temperature in the house even higher.

"I can't wait."

~~

"Are you sure your guest won't mind you stepping away to show me your house?" Levi asked.

He'd waited two hours through several board games and card games until he joined her in the kitchen where she was beginning to clean up. He'd shown up late and so the hour was already getting late. He was hoping for a moment alone with her.

"No. Trust me, they are fine without me. They'll sit all night if I don't put them out. Some of them have had a lot to drink, so they won't be getting keys back tonight. They'll either find a corner somewhere in the house to sleep or I can call them a ride. I'm about to make some coffee to sober a few of them up."

"Cool, cool. Do I get a ride if I've had too much to drink?"

"If that's what you want and need," she said, replying in jest to her playful tone. The glint in his eyes told the story.

They had watched each other the entire night. There were a few of her female friends at the party who recognized him and tried to make a play for him, but Levi, being the gentleman he is, thanked them for their many compliments, but unbeknownst to most in attendance, he had his eyes and intentions on her. He knew who and what he wanted and it was the beautiful woman standing in front of him.

"Well, if you give me that tour right now, I'll tell you what I would like and definitely what I need. How's that?"

"Would you like that tour, right now?"

"Love to. No time like the present."

Natalie walked him through the living room, which was more exquisitely designed than her family room. She decorated her living room to be looked at but not to sit in, something she got from her mother. She remembered growing up and not being able to sit in the family's living room and now she understood why. It was a room that should always be pristine and not have that lived in look like places in the house where everyone usually gathered.

"And this is my home office. I don't do any kind of work in it, but I'm hoping to get into crafting soon so this will be my workspace. I hear it relaxes you."

She was about to turn to leave when she sensed Levi leaning closer to her. She could feel his breath on the back of her neck.

"There are lots of ways to relax. Crafting is nice, but let me know if you want to hear about more ways to relax. Do I make you nervous?"

Natalie was trying hard to not let her true desire for him show. Every time she was in Levi's presence, every part of her tingled and knowing that he was interested in her had her up all night just thinking about him.

"No, not nervous. Do you really have no idea what you voice does to a woman? It's like it cascades all over. The shivering from it is uncontrollable," she admitted.

"Imagine what my touch is like?" she smiled and then looked around as they headed up the stairs.

"I have three bedrooms and two bathrooms up here."

"Can I see your room?" he asked.

When their eyes met, Levi saw what he needed to see. Natalie was just as turned on by him as he was by her. They were going to be good together.

He looked into each of the rooms, the last being her room.

"It's a mess, but this is my room."

"Mind if I go inside."

Natalie walked around him, into the room which was already lit.

"Sure, come inside," she said.

He chuckled. They were playing word games like in the car. He was ready for that.

"Can I?" he asked walking up to her as she moved back toward her dresser. When her back rested against it, he moved closer, careful to only go as far as she wanted him to go. When she looked up at him, and tilted her head, her look was inviting and he was RSVPing.

"Can you what?"

Her voice cracked and that was all he needed.

"Can I come inside. You said come inside," he repeated.

"Levi, what are we doing?" she asked quietly, looking toward the bedroom door. Anyone coming up the stairs would see them.

"No one's there. And what are we doing? What do you want to do?"

"I..I..don't know."

"Do you like me, Natalie? Because I like you a whole lot. I think we can have some fun together. I need to know what you're looking for. Do you have a man?"

"No."

"Are you looking for a relationship?"

"Not at this time, I'm not. I got out of a bad marriage less than a year ago and I'm not ready for that."

"What are you ready for?" he asked.

"Honestly?" she asked.

"Yes, honestly. I'll be honest first so that we can alleviate any confusion. I like you, I want you and I'm dying to bring you pleasure like you've never had before. That's not ego talking, that's fact. I think you're sexy and this killer body is pulling me in like a moth to a flame. I can't offer you more than some fun times because my life doesn't warrant more right now. My kids are my priority and they get all of my attention whenever they want and need it. I have time for fun and mutual satisfaction if you want that. Your turn," he said.

Moving even closer to her, he liked when she moved a little closer to him showing she could give as good as she got. He wasn't the only tease in the room.

"I would love to have some great, explosive, mind-numbing sex, no strings. I'm not looking for more than that from you and it sounds like you're not either so that's perfect."

Before she could say anything else, he leaned down to taste her lips. The first brush against her soft, supple lips was slow and methodical and immediately, bells rang out in his head and he knew he needed more. With his eyes locked on hers, he leaned in again and this time, she joined him in a fiery exchange that got hot and heavy very fast. He pulled her flush against his body as her hands gripped his shirt tight. He placed one hand behind her head and made love to her mouth. He wanted her to get a taste of just how good he knew they would be together.

As the need to breathe arose, he let go of her mouth and stepped back.

"Wow!" Natalie said.

Levi let his eyes travel from her eyes to her mouth where her finger rubbed back and forth where his lips had just been.

"Wow is right. What was that? That was a first for me. I didn't want to stop kissing you. I mean, I really didn't want to stop."

"Me either. Did you feel that spark or was it just me?" she asked.

"No, sweetness, I felt that and I can't wait to feel it again. Look, I don't hold back when I see an attractive woman that I'd like to get to know intimately. Clearly we are into each other and I don't want your guest coming in search of you since this is your party. If you really want me to be neighborly, I'll leave you my number and you can give me yours. I'm a phone call away and I can walk down the block in a few minutes. If you want to really have some fun, let's do that and let it consume us both. I love getting freaky. What about you?" he asked, rubbing her lips where his lips and her finger had just been. The moment her mouth opened a little, he let a finger slip inside and with their eyes again, never leaving each other, she sucked on his finger and his world started spinning out of control with unbridled desire. If it wasn't for her party, he would strip her and take her right against the dresser, but he wanted to take his time loving her when the time was right.

"That was good," Natalie uttered and his jeans were suddenly too tight in the crotch against his zipper.

"This is too," he said, taking her hand and placing it where she could feel just how good he was. He wanted to leave her with an image of how he could please her.

"I've never, ever been this forward with a man; never. I've never felt this free sexually like I could really explore some hot fantasies. It's easy to have them with a man like you."

"You were married. Never before?" he asked. He wondered what kind of marriage did she have.

"I'll just say it was pretty strait-laced, but he never wanted to explore, even though we were married."

"You want to explore?" he asked, taking her hand and slowly kissing and sucking on each finger, loving the soft purring sounds that came out of her mouth.

"Yes."

"I want to see your ideas of what you want to do. You set the scene. We'll play by your rules and we'll have the time of our lives when you say so. Does that work?"

Levi was ready tonight, but right now wasn't the time.

He wanted them to be all alone so that if she wanted to scream loud enough to be heard on Mars, she could.

"I want you to know that I don't really know what I'm doing, but I really want to try and show you."

Levi took her face in his hands and cupped under her chin.

"Baby, whenever you're ready, call or text me and I'll be here. I told you I'm without my kids for a few days since they are out on adventures with my sister. I've got time if you do. Call me, neighbor," he said.

When she smiled and shook her head, he leaned down and kissed her going straight to a frantic desire to mate with her tongue again. She came for him with as much vigor as he was giving to her, exactly the kind of woman he loved. He looked forward to her call.

Being Neighborly
6

Could she do it? Was her sister right that she needed to learn how to live more? Did women really make the first move on a man when all she wanted was for him to make her feel good. Standing in her room in front of the floor to ceiling mirror, Natalie looked at her naked body and saw a vision of beauty. She also saw a woman in need of a man's not, but not just any man. She needed Levi's touch. Throughout the evening, they flirted with each other and on several occasions, he alluded to the kind of night he could give her, but she would have to ask for it. She loved the back and forth and the play on words between them when no one else was listening. The ball was now in her court.

As the party started winding down, her opportunity with Levi dwindled away. She as fine playing the cat and mouse thing with him while she had a house full of guests, but now that he was leaving, she felt shy and didn't know what to say.

Her chance came when she excused herself from her guests and walked him to the door. He only lived at the end of her block, so he didn't drive to her house. She walked him as far as the end of her driveway when he turned to her, standing so close, she could feel the heat of his breath in the freezing cold of the night. She was clad in a thin jacket while he was in a brown leather bomber jacket with his hands tucked in the pockets, safe from the cold.

They faced each other and she tried to focus on his face, but her shyness won out and she looked everywhere but at him. Neither spoke now that they were alone when in the midst of the party guests, they had a lot to say to each other. She missed the wayward kitty she played for his attention and now that she had it, she didn't know what to do with it. Finally, he spoke first, though it had been short and sweet.

"I'm always up for borrowing a cup of sugar if you find you have some to spare. You have my number and you know where I am; a phone call will do it. Any day you want to check your supply and let me know if you have any, use the number. I had a good time tonight and I hope this isn't the last time I'll get an invitation to your house; party or not."

His eyes blazed through her and the heat of his stare made her want to throw caution to the wind and invite him back into her house. She'd never been that bold and even now, she found the strength to be that bold, aggressive, go for what she wanted kind of woman. Levi was letting her take the lead and all she had to do was give him a signal.

After several more seconds of silence, her moment passed.

"I'm glad you came tonight."

"Until next time," he said and he leaned over and kissed her on the cheek before turning toward his house.

She stood out there watching him as if he needed her

protective eye. Just before he moved out of her line of sight, he turned and waved at her before walking off. Her eyes had been glued to the sexy stride of his walk and the way his jeans cupped his sexy behind just right. She had imaged all that those legs could do and now, hours after her last guest was gone, she was alone in her room unable to sleep. She was too aroused to even think about sleep. She thought a hot bath would help, but that only made her want him even more.

Walking into her closet, she searched through her sexiest undergarments and found exactly what she was looking for. She pulled out and slipped on a spaghetti strap eyelash lace garter lingerie set in all black. She had purchased it at a friend's lingerie party several months ago, but had yet to have a reason to wear it. Now, was the perfect time for what she had in mind. She was going to do it. She was going to take control of her own desires to let her body get served.

Looking at herself in the mirror, she loved what she saw.

Her breasts were high and full and though the bra cup was a double d, she still more than filled the large cups. She could see the large, round dark area of her nipples through the thin lace and her desire shot up to high to even measure. She was alluring, tempting, inviting and even enticing. The only thing missing was Levi. She was soon going to remedy that.

Going into the spare bedroom where her makeup counter was, she found the perfect bright red lipstick and slowly covered her lips. There was a certain part of Levi that she couldn't wait to see covered in the red hue.

She added a pair of long eyelashes, some eyeliner and found a pair of dangling diamond earrings.

Letting her hair down, it fell around her shoulders and

she fluffed it up to give herself a wild, she-devil look.

Going back into her closet, she found a pair of sex-me pumps and slowly slid them on her feet, allowing her hands to caress her legs for added pleasure. Her eyes saw her hands, but her body felt and saw Levi's hands.

Going into that secret place in her closet that no one knew about other than her, she pulled out a box full of feathers, body oils, intimate oils and lotions, condoms, lots of them were flavored, intimate handcuffs and a blindfold. The possibilities were endless if she were really ready for the kind of night she had been imagining for a long time; ever since she moved into the neighborhood and set her eyes on Levi. It was now or never. She was dressed for the part and now all she had to do was make the call.

Grabbing what she needed from her stash of unused toys and items, she found that sexy part of her and walked the walk to the stairs, using the remote control to light candles that marked the way to her bedroom. Once downstairs, she turned off all of the bright lights she'd left on and centered her attention on the fireplace and the many candles that illuminated her great room with just enough light.

Walking over to the alarm keypad, she punched in her code to turn off the system and then walked to the front door to unlock both the inside steel door and the outside glass door.

Holding on to her nerve, she grabbed her phone and decided this was the day that she was going to finally be neighborly and see what it got her.

Finding the number she needed, she closed her eyes, summoned the wayward vixen she knew was ready to come out and play and waited for him to answer.

She heard his voice and her body purred.

"Hello, neighbor," he gruffly responded, sending sexy tremors all through her body.

She was already on the verge and he'd only spoken two words. It was the sound of his voice, sexy, deep and erotic. Everything she knew it would be.

"Hi, neighbor," she responded, soft and inviting like.

"Can I help you with something?" he asked.

"Well, I'm trying to be neighborly by offering you a cup of sugar. Would you like to come and get it now?"

"Should I knock?"

"The door is unlocked."

Without waiting for a response, she disconnected the call, found the perfect spot on top of the black and white marble kitchen counter which faced the front door. She laid all of the fun toys she'd bought downstairs with her, placed the blindfold over her eyes, crossed her legs, leaned back and waited. How much time went by she didn't know, but then she heard the front door open and her nerves kicked up. He was here.

"I came for a cup of sugar," she heard Levi say as he entered.

"I have all the sugar you could ever want or need right here. Come on in and lock the door, neighbor. There's a lot to choose from."

"Well, damn!"

Natalie smiled. She got the initial response she was looking and hoping for. She was out of character and also being the sexually free, vibrant, out-of-the box thinker, she wanted to be.

"I hope you like my version of sugar?" she asked.

"You are absolutely gorgeous. All for me?" he asked.

"Definitely. Me for you, you for me?"

She could hear him moving around her. She didn't want to lessen the heightened sexuality of the moment with her blindfold on. In her marriage, her ex-husband didn't like sexy games – he was pretty much all vanilla, missionary position and in the dark. He once told her he was insecure and so he preferred the dark. She didn't mind the dark, but she loved the idea of a blindfold, not dark by way of no lights.

"I must thank my sister for babysitting because I think this is going to be a long, sexy and very stimulating night. Blindfold? You were not kidding. I told you I want to see your fantasies on display and you did not disappoint."

Without warning, she felt his hand on her leg, down on her calf where he caresses it through the thin layer of the black, silky thigh-highs. The moment his body leaned against her leg, she wasn't able to hold in the moan that escaped her lips, all in anticipation of what was to come.

"I..I..wanted to show you the me I never let anyone see."

"And why is that?"

Natalie exhaled sharply when his words were whispered into her ear. She tried to answer, but the feel of his tongue, the pad of it gliding across her earlobe and then across the skin directly underneath of it snatched words right from her mouth.

"I've never been around a man that made me feel comfortable to share this deeply with."

"But you do with me?"

"After our phone conversation last night? Yes," she moaned.

"It did turn pretty steamy and I spent the day wondering if you would call me today. When time went on, I thought you weren't interested. If you hear a zipper, it's my jacket, not my pants, but trust me I will be getting to that. You have a lot to explore and it all delights me."

Do you mind if I pick you up?"

"No, I don't mind."

"I love the mood – candles, nice music and a sexy woman – this is my kind of evening. You know, I've been thinking about you since I saw you months ago. I don't want you to think that my interest in you just happened the other day."

"I didn't know that."

Natalie felt herself being lifted, letting her head drop back, feeling like she ruled the world.

"Now you do and I don't want this to be a one-time thing. I thought about you when I got home last night and do you know what I thought about?" he asked.

Natalie shook her head as she felt herself being lowered to the plush, red sectional in her family room.

"No."

"I thought, how can I have just a taste of a woman who turns me on like no other woman ever has; and I mean that. I got home after your party and when I hopped in the shower, you were on my mind. Do you want to know what else?"

All she could think about was how he was talking too slow. She wanted to hear it all and he better not leave a word or image out. With her blindfold on, she didn't know what he was doing, but suddenly, she felt his lips caressing her neck as he laid her back onto the chair, spreading her legs when she naturally closed them. That was her relaxed state, but she didn't want that. She wanted to go wherever he took her. She let her legs fall open as excitement shot through her. She knew the feeling would be intensified with the blindfold on. It was so different than just being in a dark room. She had to anticipate his touch and that was electrifying and salacious.

When his lips left her neck and traveled down her chest, she almost leaped of the chair when his mouth completely covered one nipple right through the lace bra. She could feel his tongue pressing against the peaked tip and she expelled an air of satisfaction. As his tongue worked it magic, she felt his hand going up the inside of her thighs and the feeling had he squirming to get even closer to his touch. His hands were magical – his lips were titillating and she was in heaven.

"You smell amazing and you didn't answer my question. Do you want to hear more?" he asked.

"Yyyess," she stammered out.

She listened expecting words, but instead, she felt him sliding down her body, kissing his way across her stomach and down to her thighs. He focused on one and then the other as he moved higher between her legs. She knew what was coming and she held her breath in anticipation. She had been married to a man who would not go down on her and that used to piss her off, but Levi was headed there about to fulfill a need, a desire she had. She tried to prepare herself and realized quickly there was no way to.

"Well, I, of course was naked in the shower, all wet and soapy and then an image of you came to me. We were in your room like we were last night. This time, I had you bent over, gripping your beautiful round ass, entering you from behind as you wiggled telling me you wanted more."

"More," she practically screamed, hoping he would keep

talking but also add action to the words. She had a place that needed him. Could she tell him it had been years since a man tasted her?

"Yes, just like that. You wanted more. Do you want more now? You know where I'm headed. You look so good to me laid out like a dinner platter for me to feast on. I want you to know that I'm taking my sweater off, not shirt underneath and I'm kicking my shoes off. I'm getting as comfortable as you look."

"I want to see?" she slurred.

"Patience, baby. First let me finish my story. Thinking of you that way had me rock hard. I was so hard that there was no way I was going to get a good night's sleep with a raging hard-on like that. I took the job in my hands literally and thought of your hands where mine were, stroking me until you pulled everything out of me. My release was so powerful that I sank to the floor in exhaustion. That's what you did for me last night and I thank you. Now, let me do something for you."

She wanted to ask what since she couldn't see, but the words were caught in her throat. Without any pretense, she felt Levi's mouth on her. He was caressing her with his tongue through the thin material of her panties; panties she already knew were soaking wet. She felt that the moment she knew he had entered her house. The idea of him had her moist for him from the start.

She squirmed about, allowing her hips to rock from side to side, taking in as much of the feeling as she could. She could feel her arms flail about the same way her head was moving. In the next second, he'd moved beyond the barrier of her panties and entered her with his tongue. She wanted to reach for his head to hold him in place, but the movement felt awkward – not knowing if he wanted that. She couldn't figure out what to do with her hands because the feelings he was pulling from her had her mind unfocused on anything other than the masterful way in which he was bringing her pleasure. Oh, how she missed oral sex. She couldn't wait to reciprocate.

As she put her hands above her head, then on her own chest and then on the chair beside her, she felt Levi reaching for her hands and he placed them on his head.

"Do whatever you want baby, even if it doesn't feel natural to you. This night is about giving you what you want and what you need. Hold nothing back," he said.

Natalie felt her essence rising above her body. She could feel herself floating, higher and higher. She opened her legs even more to give him better access and when she did, he really did feast on her like a dinner platter. He was loving her with his mouth and then she felt him add a finger along with his tongue. One of his hands slid up her body and pushed the cups of her bra up so that he could caress her large mounds, one and then the other. The feeling was so exhilarating that she could feel him all over her.

She was about to plead for more, but her body surprised her and shot off like a rocket faster than she expected. She road that wave of her orgasm and thankful for being home, she let her scream go without keeping any control. Her hips bucked up into his face and he held on tight, giving, giving and giving some more until she collapsed her hips back onto the chair, barely able to control her breathing. She'd never had a release slam into her so hard before.

She felt her blindfold being removed as Levi took it and

tossed it to the floor. When her eyes met his, the desire in them was so potent, she never wanted to look away.

She watched him quickly divest himself of the rest of his clothing while grabbing a condom from his pocket and tossing several more to the floor beside them. As he sheathed himself, no words were said. She looked at herself laid out for him and was happy that the look in his eyes said he enjoyed what he saw. She had never felt more sexy, more vibrant or more beautiful.

She tried to sit up and reach for him, hoping to please him the way he'd just done her.

"Baby, if you touch me in any way, this will be over. Not that I won't bounce right back and take us higher again and again because I will. Right now, I really need to be inside of you. I have been thinking about that since I first saw you. We have all night to get to what I think you want to do and to those toys on the counter. I haven't forgotten about those. I want you to show me what you do with them when you're alone. I think it's sexy to watch a woman pleasure herself. A man can learn a lot from what you need and desire by watching how you give yourself what you need. I have other plans for the moment."

Natalie didn't care as long as his plans involved what she was looking at. She'd seen large penises before on strippers and in porn, which she loved to secretly watch, but never has she seen a man as long and thick as Levi. There was no doubt he was nine inches and more. She loved them big; just didn't have one that big in her past. Licking her lips, she looked forward to getting a taste, but right now, she was focused on what was next.

"I love a lot of positions. What's your favorite?" he asked, leaning down, kissing her lips again and again, licking along the seam that parted her lips. When she opened for him, he dove inside allowing his tongue to search her mouth to find the pleasure points, especially on the roof of her palate and she didn't disappoint. When he touched them, she grabbed his face and went at his mouth like a starving woman. Now, he knew they were about to get even more into it.

"On my knees. I love to be on my knees," she whispered between kisses.

"Mmm, damn, you are my kind of woman. Turn over baby. I can't wait to find out about all the positions you like before the end of the night."

Natalie moved with purpose. First, she moved so that Levi could remove her panties. As she reached for the thigh-highs, he stopped her, telling her to leave them on. He loved how sexy she looked in them.

She grabbed a pillow from the chair and leaned down into him. The moment she felt him slowly working his way into her body, her teeth chattered first at the instant of pain she felt and then there was nothing but pleasure as he slid all the way in. They moved together, she pushed back into him while he pushed forward into her. She felt all of him. The feeling was out of this world. Levi made her feel full and sexy and vivacious and never again, will she accept not getting what she wanted from a man when it came to sex. It didn't have to be so vanilla.

"Yes," she shouted again and again, taking and giving to him, making sure they both got what they needed. His grunts surged her on as she felt that familiar feeling start in her thighs and then seared straight to her womanhood. She was there. As Levi increased the pace, she matched him stroke for stroke. His hands gripping her hips held them steady, but her body still flailed out of control. She slammed her eyes closed, held tight to the pillow and let go. She road the wave of delight as white lights exploded in her head.

Behind her, Levi grunted and growled with an animalistic sound that edged her on and she pushed back harder and faster until he dug his hands into her hips and howled through his own release. They mated wildly with neither of them holding back. She wanted this; she needed this and if she never had him after tonight, she was finally living out her fantasy of letting go and embracing what pleased her and right now, that was Levi.

As they calmed, she fell forward to the chair with him on top of her. The sounds of their heavy breathing overshadowed the music playing. She focused on her breathing, realizing her release had hit her so hard that she literally had to gasp for air.

"Goodness!" she yelled as Levi planted kissed all across her sweaty back.

"Natalie, if I survive this night with you, this will go down in the record books as an orgasm like none I've ever had before. I think I'm having a heart attack," he joked.

She laughed along with him.

"All I have to say is, do not have a heart attack before we get through all those condoms you threw on the floor. You didn't bring them for decorations did you because I don't know what you've done to me, but I need a lot more of you tonight. It's been a long time for me," she admitted.

"As long as I'm your neighbor and we can be neighborly, you won't have to worry about it being a long time for you again."

Natalie laughed out loud.

"Sho' you right!" she exclaimed.

~~

Levi turned and snuggled close to Natalie. Her bed was so inviting, especially with her in it. After several rounds in her family room, including her showing him what she loved to do with her collection of sex toys, he carried her upstairs where they took a shower together and she showed him how powerful her other set of lips were, draining all of his strength. They had both fallen asleep briefly. When he woke and reached for her, she went into his arms and they went another round. Looking at his phone as he held her in his arms as she stretched and purred, he knew that soon, it would be morning. They had been unable to resist each other all night and true to what she wanted, they used up four of the five condoms he'd brought with him.

"You're woke again?" Natalie asked.

"Woman, you're going to be the death of me," he joked.

"Ah, you created this sex monster that is me."

"You won't get a single complaint from me. Listen, don't read too much into this, but we have nosey neighbors. I don't want anything to seem awkward by what I'm saying. Would you like me to leave while it's dark before morning?"

"Do you want to leave?" she asked.

"Hell, no. I want to be sure I'm thinking about you and how you feel about me creeping out of here in broad daylight for everyone to see. I like you and I don't care about these neighbors. I'm only interested in one; you and how you feel about me being seen leaving here is my only concern."

"Then, stay. I have much more energy left, what about you," she quipped.

"If I'm invited to stay without creeping out like a little secret, I say, there is one condom left and I want to make the best of it."

When Natalie moved to straddle his hips, he knew they were on the same page. He was even more thankful that she locked herself out of the house and he was driving by. He would hate to miss more of her.

Being Neighborly
Epilogue

Another shift at the hospital under her belt and Natalie couldn't wait to get home. She was still reeling from those few days a week ago when she and Levi were both off from work and spent time exploring each other and their fantasies. They had talked since then and had texted quite a bit, but there had been no mentioning of more nights like those. She thought about putting another offer out on the table like she did when she invited him over for sugar, but she didn't want to assume he wanted to continue on from that time they agreed to share fantasies.

She still loved listening to his radio show every night and when he spoke and played those songs sexy songs, her mind took her back to all the ways he masterfully pleasured her and how he enjoyed allowing her to express herself like she's never done before.

Pulling into her garage, she entered the house and prepared herself for her usual routine. She started feeling a little down because she'd missed most of his show due to a last-minute emergency at the hospital. She started to grab her wine and her glass and decided instead to just grab a hot shower in place of her usual bath and catch the last few songs of his set before he got off the air.

Just as she set the alarm and headed upstairs, her cell phone pinged. Reaching for it, she smiled as she read the text from Levi:

'I know I've been busy, but I've been thinking about you. I figure by now, you would be home from work. If so, I was wondering what time you had to be to work tomorrow. It's the weekend and my kids are with my parents until Sunday evening. Would you like to come over and borrow a cup of sugar? I'm being a neighborly and stuff'

She laughed so loud, it echoed throughout her house.

'I am running short on sugar. What time do you get home?'

'I'll be about another hour. If I give you the code to my door and I can turn the alarm off from here, would you like to wait for me in my bed or any other place in my house in something hot and sexy?'

'I can do that, neighbor'

'I'll see you then, neighbor'.

Unforgettable

Baltimorean Reagan Kelly was expecting an uneventful weekend in New York City visiting her sister between Thanksgiving and Christmas. Though in the holiday spirit, the last thing she thought she'd find on a cold, wintery night was a chance at romance.

Two days in New York City for business and a chance to see his best friend was all Crime Novelist, Keith Jackson had time for, or so he thought. He soon found time to extend his stay when the chance of a lifetime to spend four incredible days with the most beautiful woman he'd ever encountered landed at his feet.

An unforgettable weekend is one thing, but can that weekend turn into a lifetime of unconditional love for Reagan and Keith, two self-professed workaholics, who didn't have a reason to slow down and smell the roses until now?

Get the next exciting installment of "The Brothers of Chi-Town" with "Crashing into Love", book 6, available in paperback and download in 2021

Joey Kincaid was all set to finally have the life he wanted as a professional wrestler. Scouts were looking at him and thanks to a family friend, he was able to showcase his talent at monthly wrestling matches at the *Montiel Avage Casino* in Chicago. Along with his brother, Carlos, the two of them were unstoppable. Just when he thought that all if his dreams were about to come through, a car crash curtailed his dreams and he was left not knowing if would ever wrestle again.

Marlow Warren was offered the job of a lifetime as a physical therapist in New York City. After growing up in Chicago, she was ready to leave one big city to trade it in for another. As she was saying her final goodbye to the city that brought her one tragedy after another, one wrong mistake behind the wheel of her car could cost a man his life and it would be her fault. She couldn't leave Chicago after that.

Never had anyone said that a car crash was the best day of their life. Joey could say it, but then Marlow's past showed up and his life was headed for another collision and this time, he wasn't fighting for his life, he was fighting for love.

Are you ready for the fire and attitude that comes with book 5 of, "The Brothers of Chi-Town" series? Come get some in "It Takes Two to Tangle"- available now.

Councilman Tucker Glass, a native of Chicago, has set his eyes on the biggest prize, that of Mayor of the city he has loved all of his life. At thirty-nine, his career spans back many years as a City Council member and then most recently, as City Council President. His resume reads like a ratings-topper novel full of accomplishments that make him more than qualified for the job, but what he wants to avoid is the drama that could block his path to the Mayor's mansion. He's always been a strait-laced politician, but his personal life could spawn a real-life reality show complete with hair pulling, tongue-lashing and accusatory finger pointing which would all occur in the first episode.

Tucker wasn't expecting his past to come back to haunt him just as he'd found the woman who was making his life complete. He would do anything to keep her in his life, but is he willing to give up his run for the Mayor's office to keep that love in-tact?

Nichelle Michaels didn't know that love could be so right until she met and fell in love with Tucker Glass, a man fourteen years older and wiser than her, but who showed her how a man should treat a woman, and that's after she spent the past year testing the water between how a man loves and how a woman loves. Now that she knows what she wants, a woman from Tucker's past could ruin her perfect love.

Tucker and Nichelle are in love, but is he willing to risk his chance at being Mayor because his ex-wife, or the woman he thought was his ex-wife, wants to now be First Lady of Chicago? Was he really ready to tangle with a woman who specialized in drama every day on television as the star on the nation's number one reality show?

Tucker may be ready for Chicago, but is Chicago ready for the drama that comes along with the popular politician?

FBI Agent, Quintin Bell was sent to work undercover at Tee King Investment Securities to get proof that Carlos King, owner and hedge-fund boss, was embezzling money from his own employees' retirement accounts. In a chance encounter, he noticed Carlos' daughter, Meadow and before he could keep his heart from getting lost in her beauty, he found himself at a crossroads between doing his job and following his heart.

Meadow King wasn't looking for love that day in the café, but there was no way she could resist the handsome, rugged looks of a stranger when the intoxicating vibe between them became undeniable and irresistible. Unbeknownst to Meadow, the man she's fallen in love with has a secret that could not only ruin the love that grew between them, but it could topple her entire world.

Quintin knows that love can be real and it can be true, but his lies are what create a façade of their love affair and could cause it to crash and burn just as it has begun to heat up with passion that neither of them had ever experienced before nor could they see themselves without ever again. Quintin is running out of time in trying to find a way to do his job and hold on to the woman he loves. His biggest hurdle will be if he does his job, can he convince Meadow that his lies may have been true, but his love is truer!

Book 1, "Heartthrob" of "A Lovers' Heart Series

Get it on Kindle Unlimited as a free read!

Cade Weston, Hollywood's most eligible bachelor and named the world's sexiest man of the year, lives life at the top with a bevy of beauties at his beck and call, people providing his every desire and more money than any one person should have.

Callie Hurston struggles to make it as a stylist to the stars in a world where women are intimidated by her beauty and men are interested in her body and not her talent. Cade thought he had it all until he has a chance meeting with Callie and decides to take a chance on her talent and ends up taking an even bigger chance with his heart. Can the playboy turn in his player's card and give in to love?

Book 2, "Heartbeat" of "A Lovers' Heart Series

In book two of, "A Lovers' Heart" series, Navy SEAL, Calvin Lymon, was about his country's business when he allowed himself to cross the line and his heart got involved resulting in a love lost. Injured in the line of duty, he fights to stay alive for the sake of his newborn son, Camico.

A new city and a new outlook on life were exactly what physical therapist, Ava Cortez, needed after years of living life alone and off the grid to avoid being detected by a madman. She never allowed herself to love anyone, especially a man, afraid she would be found out. When she's asked to oversee the therapy of a sexy navy SEAL, she tries to fight the immediate and intoxicating lure to a man who exudes more sexual potency than she's ever experienced. Can she forget about business and indulge in pleasure for once?

Calvin deals with the days of therapy that drain him, but nothing compares to the salacious, steamy nights of passion with Ava that are having the biggest impact on his ability to get back to reality until an old rival resurfaces and threatens his life and his loves.

Once and for all, Calvin knows he has to deal with his past and risk losing his woman and his son, who are his heartbeats.

In book 3, of "A Lovers' Heart" steamy romance series, Cameron Lymon, the sexy, youngest brother of Hollywood heartthrob, Cade Weston and Navy SEAL, Calvin Lymon, with his Master's degree in Journalism and a minor in Communications and Sports Management in hand, landed his dream job in Denver, Colorado as the co-host for a new morning talk show. Women love to call him the *"Heartbreaker"* because of the bevy of beautiful ladies he's left in his wake, not interested in giving up being a bachelor for falling in love. He enjoys taking after his big brother's old lifestyle of being a playboy.

Dakota Kane sacrificed a personal life and fought hard in her career to be the lead personality on Denver's top television morning show, but she was about to risk it all for passionate, steamy encounters with her new, much younger co-host, who is ten years younger and fifty shades hotter than any man she'd ever encountered. All he had to do was smile at her and she was a goner.

Cameron didn't know what he was in for when what he thought would be casual, behind closed door romps with the ever-so-sexy Dakota began to turn into much more when his heart became as invested in her as much as his body had. As things turned serious, his heartbreaker status came back to haunt him and his relationship with Dakota was threatened by his past.

Cameron and Dakota have to decide if what they are beginning to feel for each other is worth the risk of their careers when their secret love affair becomes the topic of public opinion and ridicule.

A Designed Affair

In this follow-up to "Bachelor Not for Sale", Loren Knight has been engaging in a secret love affair with her brother Duron's best friend and business partner, Michael Bailey. He is everything she could want and more in a man, but she believes the risk is too great for any type of relationship with him beyond their steamy encounters behind closed doors.

Michael Bailey has been fighting his attraction to Loren for years. He has stayed away from her out of respect for his best friend and business partner. Now that he and Loren have finally given into the passion they have been craving, can Michael convince Loren that what they share is worth the risk of even Duron finding out?

When I Think of You

Leo Westmoreland is an ordinary guy living in Harlem, New York, working three jobs to make ends meet the best way he can in order to take care of his family years after his abusive father disappeared from their lives. He's kept romance on the back burner, but that's all about to change.

Raquel Johnson was born with a silver spoon in her mouth to a father who owns one of the top money management firms in Manhattan. Though she's never wanted for anything, she's made her own achievements in life and now sits as an executive with his company. Her dating life has consisted of men who value money, power and prestige over unconditional love, the one thing she desires the most. Leo and Raquel meet and share a connection that breathes new life into them and proves that focusing on each other and the love they can have together is more important than anything else.

Black Love

Dawson Frazier stood on the sideline and watched the woman of his dreams get mistreated and disrespected by his philandering best friend, the man she was about to marry. He wanted to step in and rescue her, but he didn't want her coming to him that way.

Riley Cooper was left at the altar, confused and embarrassed by the man she thought loved her. It took her over a year to get over that disappointment and with the help of a good man, she was able to see what it really meant to love and to be loved.

About the Author

Cheryl Barton lives in Maryland and in her spare time she loves to read espionage, crime and romance novels, cook, watch Sci-fi movies, spend time with family and friends and enjoy Maryland steamed crabs. Cheryl is celebrating 30 years as a government employee and loves writing romance novels when she's not working. Cheryl is the author of 31 romance novels, 3 inspirational novels and is proud of 4 book compilation projects with several other incredible women called, "One Sister Away: Encouraging Words from One Sister to Another" – a series of books meant to encourage, empower and inspire other women. People often ask Cheryl which book is her favorite of all of those she's written. While she finds it hard to select one favorite, Cheryl still looks to her first novel, Bachelor Not for Sale, if she had to pick a favorite because it was her first novel and the one that inspired her to continue writing.

Cheryl was a 2019 Finalist for the Emma Award given by Romance Slam Jam and a 2018 Finalist for the Literary Trailblazer of the Year award by the Indie Author Legacy Award. Cheryl is a member of the Romance Writers of America – National Chapter, the Maryland Romance Writers and the Contemporary Romance Writers groups, the Black Writers' Guild of Maryland and the International Women Writers Guild.

Connect with Cheryl Barton

www.cherylbarton.net
www.crbarton.com
www.amazon.com/author/cherylbarton

Instagram: @cherylbartonbooks
Twitter: @cbartonbooks
Facebook: @cherylbartonbooks